A TALE
OF
BLOOD
AND
TEARS

SHADOWED TIME

TIME

‣BOOK ONE‧

ROBERT SCHECK

Credit to the Editor: Warren Layberry
Credit to the Designer: Gabrielle Ragusi

Paperback ISBN: 978-1-0880-7530-2

Acknowledgments

Without the following people, the story you now hold in your hands, poised to read for your own pleasure, would not be possible. Through the incredible work of my initial editor, who spent countless hours poring over my manuscripts and finding most every mistake that I glossed over, this book is now available to be read by all.I'd also like to thank—in memoriam—my little brother, Simon Scheck. The inspiration I drew from him formed the basis for much of what I put into Phoenix Rather. Simon's good heart and outgoing energy is what grips the soul of Phoenix in this first installment of the Blood & Tears saga.Although they populate this text, I'd be remiss if I did not remember all those who interacted with me and provided inspiration for the characters you are about to meet. Many individuals from my life have made it into this book through the characters' voices, and I thank them.Finally, I'd like to thank you, the reader, in advance, for taking the time to read this book. Behind every author there abides a mighty force of readers.

Contents

Of the golden halls, none shall remain—
of the weeping city, all shall fade.
The tales of glorious man shall cease,
and the age of the Elfin perish beneath ere
the return of Mordën in darkness upon Ëonë
in the soul of a bairn
in shadowed crossing o're the misty aisle.

1 ▸ Darkness On The Western Front

Crisp leaves crunched under my sneakers as I walked along the brick path. I kicked at a pile of maple pods. A startled mouse skittered away and dove into a sewer pipe, which belched a combination of black smoke and acrid stench. A school bus weaved through parked cars as it traveled along the recently paved road.

The fall day was unusually cool, even for Colorado, and my breath ballooned in front of me as I walked. Grey clouds crossed the sky and cast shadows that made patterns on the ground, which were not—if imagination was heavily applied—unlike animal forms. The day, despite the decreasing temperature and lack of sunshine, was quite pleasant. It was a nice break from the odorous, steaming summer hours which had plagued much of Clearwater during the past several weeks.

My walk to school was by far the most enjoyable part of the day. All around the trees boasted vibrant colors of gold yellows, blood reds, and sea greens. As I walked, leaves fluttered in spirals and circles to the ground. I crunched the fallen leaves which lay carpeted before me. The soft music from my earphones made me smile. I was content.

A soft growl rattled me and yanked my mind from thoughts of autumn and plunged it back to reality. The growl intensified, and for a moment I feared a dangerous dog was approaching. The nervousness abated when I saw a small white poodle. The dog peered at a squirrel as it chattered noisily.

So much for *that* possible mauling. I exhaled, focusing back on my heart and settling it down. Butterflies, my mom always said of fluttering hearts and nervous stomachs, for I had always been an anxious kid.

I used to lie in bed, kept awake by dreams of what the world was turning into. Horrible nightmares of losing those I loved battled the dreamless sleep which rarely came.

My mind drifted to the recent kidnappings that had rocked the town. A news article published the day before had read:

STUDENT KIDNAPPINGS SHAKE CLEARWATER
Reporter Christosis O'Hare

Thousands across Colorado have been shocked by the sudden kidnappings in Clearwater of two young ladies from their high school campus during their prom. The kidnapper, described by witnesses as a thin, man all in black who forced the two girls into his car. The girls' prom escorts later told police that they had been getting drinks from the punch line when they heard the girls' screams. The police department has refused to divulge any information at this time but does encourage anyone with any piece of information that could lead to the arrest of this criminal to either step forward or call the anonymous tip hotline.

Sweat slicked my palms, and I rubbed them against my torn jeans. My backpack felt slightly heavier than before—the bright beautiful morning had an unsettling air of menace to it. The sound of sneaker against concrete caused me to stop dead. I whirled around. My notebook slipped out of my hands and caught onto my earbud cord, yanking it out of my ear. Six boys hurried up. Big Beef followed after them. The school bully, Big Beef, found his enjoyment in torturing girls and boys unfortunate enough to be smarter than him. No one knew his real name, save for teachers, and these he had blackmailed. Most students just call him BB. His face glistened with sweat. His grease-slicked hair was kept back by a tattered ball cap. His goons spread out behind him.

BB had a playful look in his brown eyes. He sized me up and signaled to his followers to encircle me.

"Hey BB," I said, hoping that my terror was not obvious.

He grinned. "Hey Phoenix."

My heart rate spiked. BB never used a person's name. His usual battle plan was to insult you in some particularly harsh way till you burst into tears.

I glanced about frantically, hoping that someone would see what was about to happen, and maybe intervene. Normally, the steady drone of cars and blaring buses that drove up the residential street would have been reassuring—something to be casually drowned out with earbuds and Robert Simon's "Thousand Spotlights." Now, however, the noise seemed to diminish altogether, and I could only hear BB's snarling voice.

"What do you think you're doing?" The smell of cigar smoke hit me. "School is on the next street over, so me and my buddies here would like to know what you're doing on my turf!"

I tried not to show fear. Letting a bully like BB sense that his intimidation was succeeding would be like dumping blood in shark infested waters, then hopping in naked. I opened my mouth to spout some defiant retort.

"Oh, uh well... I, uh—"

"You're so pathetic." He put his big hands on my chest and shoved me backward. "I could beat you raw with both hands tied behind my back." He and his buddies thought that was quite funny.

"Oh come on guys," I said, for a brief moment exasperation overriding my fear, "is he seriously the best you could come up with?"

My bravery resulted in a punch to the gut. I gasped and dropped to both knees, slammed my fists on the sidewalk, and gagged. BB snorted with laughter. I staggered back to my feet, raising my hands in a weak attempt at a fighting posture. Before I realized what was happening, I found myself laid out flat. A dull throb began in my head, and I tasted blood where I had bitten into the side of my cheek. BB kneed me in the gut.

"What's the matter?" He snarled, his face an inch from mine. He yanked hard on my shirt collar. "Can't handle yourself in a fight?" He hoisted me up. I shook my head to clear it. Spots spiraled across my vision, and the previously stationary world began to undulate in dizzying colors. I readied myself to be rendered unconscious.

"I haven't heard an apology yet." He turned to his henchmen. "Have you guys heard an apology yet?"

I cried out as he twisted my arm behind my back. The others behind him shook their heads

"I've dreamed of destroying you," I murmured, but he didn't hear me.

During the brief tussle of silence and pain, I tried to think of a tactic to break his concentration just enough so that his grip would slacken.

I kicked out violently. Big Beef may have been known for being the strongest, cruelest kid in the high school, but he was also by far the slowest. It took him a moment to register where my Converse sneaker was headed. The second of hesitation was all I needed.

He yelped in pain, doubling over. His hands went to his midriff. I barreled up the sidewalk, his minions hot on my trail. I only hoped the prey could outrun the predators.

"Get him!" BB bellowed. "Get him and drag him back here."

I was about to give up all hope—the grasping fingers of my pursuers a few inches from fastening on my shirt—when I saw someone across the street. She was engrossed in a book. The girl lifted her head slightly, caught sight of me and frowned.

The boys stopped and retreated as she strolled over. I sighed with relief although my insides squirmed with the pain BB had wrought.

"This is not over," BB screeched in the distance. "You hear me, you little rat?"

My pulse would have quickened at the approach of the girl if I hadn't already felt like I'd run a marathon. Katherine Chase, my savior, had been my childhood best friend as far back as I could remember. We'd grown up together and shared our dreams for the future. Recently, I'd begun to notice a change in my feelings whenever she was around me. She spent more time with her nose in her books of mystery than she did anything else. It was one of the many reasons I couldn't help but feel drawn to her. Today, she had been engrossed in a novel called *The Shady Arachnid's Ruination.*

"Hey Phoenix." Katy smiled, stopping before me. She turned to face where the others had vanished. "BB can be such a jerk. I've tried telling the principal, but he just tells me to keep my... Phoenix? Do I have something in my hair?"

I realized I'd been staring at her, mouth slightly open. The sun caught her in a wreath of golden light, and her blonde hair, and the fragrance of her perfume had caught me by surprise.

"Jerk?" I said, shaking my head as though I hadn't just been caught gaping at her. I glanced theatrically over my shoulder. "Try future inmate at Clearwater County Jail." I hoped I sounded suave and not like a complete idiot. "How are you?"

Her cheeks were flushed pink from the cold, and she wore a white shirt and a pink skirt. Her hair was slung over her shoulder in a ponytail; the faint whiffs of lilac-scented shampoo still lingering.

I felt my face reddening. Bad enough that I had to be humiliated by the biggest kid in our school, but to have Katy see it just rubbed salt in the wound.

"Come on, you! Walk me to school?" She slipped her book inside her bag and slung it over one arm.

If I hadn't blushed before, this question really did the trick. For another few seconds I stammered until I could remember who I was.

"Oh, absolutely." I grinned.

She gave me another huge smile and began to walk toward

school, her ponytail bouncing up and down. A glow seemed to surround her. She turned slightly and glanced back. Her full lips parted in slow motion...

I love you, Phoenix.

I stumbled into a trashcan and did a full flip onto the ground, landing on my back. Amidst the pencils and books and trash that had scattered on the ground, I found my pride and dignity and stood up.

"Are you coming," she said, a bemused look on her face, "or would you rather BB got you?'"

Trying to act like flipping over a trashcan was perfectly normal; I brushed the leaves off my shirt.

We began the trek in silence, but it soon became evident that Katy could not hold back a tidal wave of information as she lectured on about the predictability of modern novels.

"... and in every book I read, the main protagonists always come out alive in the end. I think authors need to start formulating new plots where more centralized characters meet their own demise. I mean, sure, there's George R.R. Martin, but he's almost the exception that proves the rule, and fantasy has always played by slightly different rules to begin with. What about non-genre works..."

Her words began to flow together in a soup of arguments and counterarguments. I found myself stealing glances at her.

"What about if you were in a book?" I turned her thought around. "You wouldn't want to die at the hands of some evil villain, would you?"

"I'm happy then that this is not a fictional world." She giggled. "If it was who knows what might happen?"

Overhead, a flock of Canada geese flew in formation, honking their way past a grove of spruces and out of sight. Nose quivering to the scents of the world, a rabbit lay crouched in the grass of an unkempt lawn, nibbling at green blades. Copses of trees, some still clinging to the last hopes of fall, sported empty nests and the occasional bird. In one house we passed, a boy had his nosed smeared to the glass, eyes glued to a mail truck which had just pulled up.

"My biggest pet peeve is that authors think they are being creative when in reality all they are doing is stealing original ideas and making them unoriginal. Someone has to write a book where at least one of the important and vital characters die! Death is crucial."

When I didn't say anything, she glanced at me out of the corner of her hazelnut-colored eyes.

"What?" I mumbled. "Oh yeah."

"You're really distracted today." Katy tilting her head to the side, observing me closely. "Anything wrong? Don't tell me Casey has been making fun of you again? I told you when she does that you need to stand up to her."

Of course, something is wrong, I'm walking with you and I can't seem to create a sentence without looking like a dork.

I cleared my throat. "Casey has been the least of my worries. I'm still shaky over my encounter with BB. That guy sure knows how to intimidate. Think they have a class for that? If so, it would be the only class he could get an A in."

She laughed, a sound like chimes tinkling in the wind, and touched my arm. I froze.

"On the serious side though," she said, "you can't allow him to keep accosting you like this. One of these days you'll have to stand up to him."

"Oh, I'll stand up to him!" I shook my fist in the air then slowly lowered it. "I'll stand up to him alright when I'm four feet taller, weigh twice as much as he does, and have my own unicorn."

"Well so long as you have a plan." She winked, bounding ahead and twirling.

I checked my watch and was about to tell her that we should hurry as homeroom would begin soon, when a group of girls marched in unison from a side street, their flamboyantly pink hair made them immediately recognizable. Claire Blog, the lead cheerleader and all-around snob, was almost as cruel as BB although her method of torture manifested in the form of words, not brawn. Katy had recently joined the cheerleading squad and Claire considered her teammates to be wasting time if they weren't practicing every possible hour of the day.

Claire flashed me a look that probably was meant to appear sympathetic, as if she cared, but only carried the message that I shouldn't be with Katy. Thankfully, I was used to those looks and, in fact, expected them. You don't spend all of middle school and two years of high school being shunned by most of the girls and not get used to it.

"Hey Katy," she droned, chewing a piece of gum and squinting her eyes. "You should walk with us. No offense of course, Phoenix." The way she said 'Phoenix' was almost like it was a dirty word. "I heard your dad lost his job. How long before you have to leave the school? It's only for like, um, kids with a lot of money, you know?"

"You heard wrong. My dad hasn't lost his job, so yes, Claire, I am still going to this school."

"Katy, come on!" She glared at me and tossed her braided hair back over her shoulder.

Katy gave me a shy, apologetic smile before she hurried off, book bag clutched in one hand. Once again, I was left alone.

The rest of the walk to school was monotonous. Not even the smiles as a group of young toddlers toddled past could make me feel better. I held my breath and felt a heavy weight settle back into place.

The buzzer for homeroom sounded right as I strolled into the long hallway that housed our lockers. I pulled out my history book and raced off to class. Mr. Grizwald had been in the process of closing the door. He stared at me and opened the door just wide enough for me to squeeze past.

"Thank you for showing up, Mr. Rather," he drawled, his speech thick with the accent of a native-born Southerner. "In the future, may I advise you to arrive ten minutes prior to homeroom or I shall be forced to give you a detention slip."

I removed my backpack and stuffed myself behind my desk. Snorting, BB sprawled in his chair half in and half out.

This was going to be a really long and really tedious morning.

▲▼▲▼▲

The school buzzer sounded three hours later, and pandemonium erupted as kids leapt out of their stupors, clashing together, their backpacks and hands a blur as they all tried to be the first out of the room.

"Do not forget that tomorrow we will be covering algebraic functions!" Mr. Stark, our math teacher, called after them. "Your exam will follow that half-day lecture." His voice grew lost in the excited babble of teens pushing for the lunchroom.

I stood and shoved my schoolbooks into the black hole of my backpack, pausing to gaze at the black widow spider etched into the fabric. I reached out and ran a finger over the coarse stitches.

"Hey Dog, you seem down." The smooth voice broke me out of my reverie.

I turned and smiled as one of my best friends sauntered up, his phone in one hand and his backpack in the other.

Tim Brestdon was roughly six feet tall, broad shouldered, with thick dreadlocks draped around his shoulders. He was one of those guys destined to be either a heavy weight champion or a linebacker.

He pulled his ever-present earbuds out and waggled his fingers. Sporting a football jersey, Tim pulled his hat down. Winking at a passing girl and dodging the pencil eraser she threw at him, he slouched against the wall.

The room emptied within the next minute, and we shuffled off to the cafeteria. The halls rang with the loud chattering of kids gossiping. Locker doors slammed shut as textbooks were tossed in and phones were brought out.

"What's good, fam?" Tim nodded as he draped his earbuds around his neck.

"Trying to get over the fact that I failed the history exam. Dude, Christopher gave me a C. I studied for this exam forever. I even got Katy to help me."

"Hey man, Chris goes hard on everyone. I got an A on that exam but only because it was multiple choice. When in doubt, chose C. Anyways, Simon and the guys are going to play basketball after lunch," he said. "Wanna chance your luck in there too? I hear the competition is going to be tough."

I wanted to give an emphatic "yes" as the basketball courts in our gym tended to be overly crowded. However, Will had already asked me to go over homework with him on my lunch period.

"Maybe." I shrugged.

"Cool!" Tim chuckled, his locks swinging side to side. "See ya there. Don't chicken out on me, man!"

And with that, he was away.

"Where are you going?" I called back, surprised. Tim was like that sometimes.

He melted into the mob of students streaming toward the cafeteria. Only his dreadlocks could be seen floating along. I shrugged and picked up my backpack and cast it over one arm. Weighed down, I stumbled out the classroom door.

When I finally made it into the noisy lunchroom, I halted. One thing I always appreciated was the careful inspection and dedication to duty that the staff had. Not a floor went ignored, not a food stain untouched, not a table nor window was left dirty. The result was a clean environment to eat my lunch in. I checked for the unwanted presence of bullies—surprisingly they were absent. Maybe today wouldn't be that bad.

I eyed the entire room and saw Katy sitting with Claire and her entourage of girls at a corner table. Katy nibbled a carrot; a depressed look clouded her eyes.

I dropped my bag onto the floor next to a plastic table and slid in. The loud drone of students soon became background noise, and I breathed in slowly, once again practicing my calming routine. I shoved an earbud in, closed both eyes, and was beginning to jam out when I felt another presence next to me.

"Hey Phoenix." Will's voice.

I opened my eyes. If Tim was destined to be a football player, Will was destined to be the next Mark Zuckerberg. His knack for coding and hacking at blinding speed had come in handy on more than one occasion. He was dressed in his Stand Strong and Be the Nerd shirt. His buzz-cut hair and wide glasses often earned him derogatory nicknames.

"Hey dude. You didn't happen to get a C on Christopher's exam too, did you?" I asked hopefully, dumping a handful of chips into my mouth.

"I got a hundred percent. Catch the action at the tether ball courts?"

He slid across from me and opened the brown lunch sack which his mom had packed. I often envied what he was given. My lunch consisted of an apple, peanut butter and banana sandwich, and bag of chips. Where my mom went for practicality, Will's mom went for over the top emphasis. Will dumped out a bag of cookies, two lettuce and ham sandwiches with cheese and tomato, and a large bottle of colored liquid.

"Nah," I said. "Christopher had me cleaning the blackboards, so my morning was booked. Did you catch Tim's invitation to the courts?"

"Yeah." Will shrugged. He opened his bag and crammed two Oreos in simultaneously. "I told him no way. I'm busy with computer science."

My eyes strayed over to Katy's corner. She seemed so unhappy as she pushed her food around with a carrot stick. Behind her table, and chatting to the janitor, was a figure with a low cap over his face.

"Who's that?" I asked.

"New security guard, I think," Will muttered, his eyes glued to his textbook. "After the abductions, people are unsafe, and when they are unsafe, they turned to hired muscle."

"I wouldn't call a security guard *hired muscle* exactly.," I rolled my eyes. "Also, how do you know who I even pointed to?" I raised an eyebrow. "Why does he look like he came out of some fantasy book?"

"The guy has been the talk of the day. Apparently, he arrived a while ago at the principal's office. A lot of meaningless speculation that will no doubt evolve into a story void of factual basis."

I had lost Will to some higher plane. The hooded figure turned and stared at me—a pair of sunglasses masked his eyes. He hurried out of the cafeteria.

"Will, don't you think there is something off about him?"

"Would you relax? You sound like everyone else." Will grumbled, taking his attention off his book. "It's just your paranoia. I knew I should have stolen your newspaper before you could read that abduction article. The odds of someone abducting you specifically are next to none. Maybe your life is just so dull and monotonous that you create these scenarios to escape. It's sort of like my fascination with the effects of the moon on the tide. You could look it up as a better outlet."

"Moon's effect on the tide... are you serious? Dude, you know I don't do that boring stuff!"

For a moment I could see the hurt look on Will's face and immediately felt regret. His face had flushed, eyes averted to the floor.

"Dude, I'm sorry, I didn't mean..."

BB and his company of ruffians entered the cafeteria. Massive bulk a hindrance to the exiting flow of students, BB stared down anyone who made eye contact. In doing so, a circle began to form around him.
"I am so dead!" I hissed, scrunching down.

"Well, while it is true the moon's tide could have big impacts

on our sea if it somehow went away, the odds of that happening
are—"

"Dude, stop talking about tides and odds. BB just tried to
wipe the concrete with my brains this morning on the way to
school. Last thing I want is for the lunch staff to have to clean
me off the floor too!"

The school bully yanked a passing freshman out of the
flow of bodies. He began to snarl at the boy until he received
a few dollar bills. The freshman slunk out of the room, casting
shamed looks at anyone who looked at him.

"I'm booking it," I whispered, sliding out from the bench. I
reached for my backpack but didn't make it far when BB's ugly
mug swiveled. I froze.

"I have some homework to catch up on. Mrs. Mop assigned
an exorbitant amount of calculus," Will muttered.

"Will, please don't leave," I croaked as BB drew within
earshot. "You don't even need to study for calculus!"

"Hey," BB said as if he was merely concocting a conversation
and not planning how to spread my guts over the cafeteria floor,
"I've got a problem to settle. My fist wants a date with your face.
Now!"

"I uh don't think they are right for each other," I stammered,
forcing a weak grin. "Besides, I like my face, and I can be the
jealous type."

"Quit yammering," he said. "Your pretty little girlfriend
isn't going to rescue you now. When I'm done with you, you'll
wish you'd been knocked senseless back before school started."

I tried to slip past him in a desperate bid for freedom,
but his hand snagged my collar, stopping me cold. Gagging, I
felt the blood rush to my face. Faces turned and the cafeteria
quieted as everyone realized what was occurring. Claire and her
gals had stopped and were smirking. Only Katy seems to stare
at me with compassion and worry. I tried a weak smile.

"Hey, did I say you could leave?" BB twisted my arm behind
my back.

A second before I became the next cafeteria floor stain, Mr. Grizwald walked into the room, calculating the toxicity of the scene. BB released my arm. He leaned in and I felt his rank tobacco breath on my neck.

"I will find you someday soon, Phoenix. When I do, you'll regret everything."

I tried my best to look nonchalant. "Say what you will," I said adjusting my shirt, "but you're nothing but words."

I didn't like the look of the smile he gave me in return.

Mr. Grizwald broke the tension in the room. "I never received your report, BB. It was due yesterday, and you keep putting it off. I want it on my desk now. I am done with your excuses!"

I had found my escape path. While the dumb brute was being chastised, I made a beeline and left the lunchroom, my mind tired. Two interactions with BB had left me exhausted. Will had long since slipped out, but I knew where to find him. When in doubt, think it out.

The brisk stroll to Will's calculus class gave me the much-needed time I desired to calm down. Students milled around me, sharing the latest gossip and wondering who had a crush on who. I pushed open the lab door and walked in. The classroom slowly filled with returning students, so I had to make this quick. Will was working at a computer. He looked up as I entered.

"How did the interaction go?" he asked. "I haven't heard the ambulance sirens going and, based on the fact that you're here before me, gather you didn't die."

"He's nothing but hot breath. He talked himself into a corner until Grizwald found him. He won't be seeing the light outside this school until he turns in some homework assignment."

There was a short musical tone, then the crackly voice of Mrs. Shade, the school secretary, came over the PA system: Phoenix Rather, report to the principal's office right away please."

"Oh man," Will chuckled, leaning back in his seat, "who did you terrorize this time?"

I hoisted my backpack onto my shoulder and walked out of the lab. My footfalls echoed in the corridors. I turned a corner and found myself facing two doors. One led to the principal's office. The other led to the janitor's closet. My soft knock on the closed door of the principal's office sent a deep hum inward. The door slowly opened, and Mrs. Shade stood over me, glasses perched on the bridge of her nose. She looked me over twice without saying a word.

I sniffed.

She wrinkled her nose and gestured for me to enter. "Come, on. Hurry!"

I tried for a winning smile, failed, and walked into the outer office area. Principle Laroche's office door was cracked open, and I could hear the faint sounds of someone's worried voice inside. My stomach clenched.

I followed the secretary as she walked across the room and knocked softly on the door. The voices inside ceased, and the squeak of a chair as someone rose.

Mrs. Laroche opened the door fully and nodded to the secretary before she smiled kindly at me. I entered the tidy office and immediately felt claustrophobic. I had never been sent to the principal's office before, but as the saying goes there was a first for everything.

That's when I looked past Mrs. Laroche's shoulder and noticed the other person in the office.

"Mom?" What was she doing here?

Mom raised her head, her eyes were full of sadness, her face pale. She opened her mouth to say something but closed it again. I squirmed awkwardly, wondering whether I was expected to stand or sit in the only available chair.

Mrs. Laroche eased back down in her giant office chair, motioning for me to sit. Mom breathed in deeply and turned to me. Her sweater was unbuttoned, and the pockets had been crammed full of tissues.

"Hello, dear," she attempted a weak smile. "I'm sorry to pull you from your classes today."

Mom broke off and blew her nose on a used tissue. Mrs. Laroche peered at me, her gold rimmed glasses focused her laser like stare.

"Mister Rather, I have brought you here to take you out of school for an indefinite period of time."

Her voice lacked sympathy and struck me as ominous, as if she were issuing a prophecy that wouldn't bode well for me.

"I don't understand," I said. "What's happening? If this is about my grade on the previous exam, I can explain."

Mom rose and grasped my shoulder. Her skin felt ice cold.

"Mom?" It was like I was expected to know the answers without knowing the question.

"There have been some... complications with your dad's work. I need you to come with me. Mrs. Laroche has kindly agreed to let me remove you from classes until at least the end of the semester."

"Complications?" More questions than answers bubbled up, urging to be the first out. "I don't understand. What happened?"

"If you need to tell your friends goodbye, I'll let you do that." She stopped to hiccup.

"You're not answering my question, Mom." I shook my head as if to clear away some unseen fog. "What has—"

"If you don't mind," Mrs. Laroche said, "I have some office meetings scheduled, and I don't wish to fall behind here. I appreciate the talk, Mrs. Rather." Her eyes darted between the two of us, an unmistakable invitation issued to vacate her office.

"Phoenix, we are leaving, *now!*" Mom's voice had turned crisp.

The abrupt change stopped me in my tracks. Outside the open window, the distant wail of a siren wafted in. Mom picked up her purse. I rose as well. We ran into Will and Tim who were chatting next to their lockers. I paused, glancing uncertainly between them and my mother. She nodded slightly and walked out the front doors.

I turned to face Will and Tim. "Where's Katy?"

As I spoke, footsteps rushed up behind me. Katy had changed out of her outfit she'd been wearing earlier and now wore her pink and gold cheerleader skirt and top. Cheerleader practice happened after lunch period. She looked concerned.

"Phoenix? Is everything okay?"

"Um," I fumbled for the right words, "I'm leaving school. I don't know when I'll be back."

Tim looked gravely at me, a look I'll never forget. I shook his hand and turned to Katy. She had her arms folded and gave me a hopeful smile.

"I'll see you back home, I guess." I tried to cough out a shaky laugh.

▲▼▲▼▲

Mom and I pushed through the doors of school and stepped out into the bright parking lot. I slipped into the passenger side of our jeep, barely registering the new-car smell. Dad had just bought it for their anniversary. I shut the door with a weak pull and glanced out my window. My friends gathered on the school steps, Katy with one hand above her eyes to shield from the sun, while Will gave me an encouraging thumbs up.

Mom took out her keys and turned it over in the ignition. The car rumbled to life, and I waved to my friends. They turned and entered the school. We pulled out of the school lot and began cruising up to speed along a stretch of gravel road.

A beautiful day bloomed around me as I inhaled the smell of fall. Trees bordered the road as if they had parted to allow us through. The anxiety which coursed through my veins seemed like lead, weighing me down.

"I was called in to your father's work this morning," Mom broke the silence as she turned onto the main highway. A semi barreled past and the driver hit the horn—we swerved.

"I had no reason to think anything had happened." She drove in continued silence for a mile. "When I received the call, I got into the car and drove over to his work. The gate guard gave me some hassle. You know, I never liked your father's work very much."

"What actually happened?" I said. "Why have I just been removed from school?"

But she continued as though I hadn't said anything.

"I parked the car and got out only to be accosted by police." Her voice cracked as she forced herself to speak. "They asked me who I was, so I told them. They proceeded to inform me that your father was unaccounted for and that there had been a level five security breach, which is what they call it when an employee steals information from the company with intent to sell or distribute to competitors. They interrogated me for details all this morning until I told them I needed to leave and pick you up."

"What did you do next?" I sat on the edge of my seat, like I was a worried six-year-old waiting in earnest to hear the next chapter of their favorite book. "How did you find out about what was going on?"

"I persuaded them to tell me," she said. "Apparently, an employee, who they refused to name, had tried to gain access. He was turned away at the door. Ten minutes later, your father's window was shattered, and an alarm went off. The first person into his office claimed your father was nowhere to be seen. He's been missing since. They let me into the office, and before I left, I noticed a letter on his desk, fluttering in the breeze."

She handed me a small rolled piece of paper, yellowed with age. A coiled string kept the paper from unravelling. I slowly twisted it away, letting the faded edge fall as gravity claimed it. The words were scrawled in a dark ink, pressed firmly into the page.

The Hourglass, servants of Mordën, were here!

"Hourglass? Mordën?" My throat was parched. "I don't understand, Mom what does—"

"We should have told you," she said. "When you were older, I mean. But at the time, well, we just shrugged it off."

"What are you talking about?"

"It was a long time ago," she said softly, "right after you were born. We'd just put you down and you were asleep, or what passed as sleep with a newborn in the home, and there was a terrible storm. I remember the rain sheeting against the windows. We were trying to grab some sleep ourselves, and there was a pounding on the front door. Your father and I went to answer it. The storm was still raging, and your father thought someone had gone off the road or something. When we opened the door there was this... dark form. He was just standing there the wind at his back and rain pouring off of him. Your father asked what was wrong, and we'd have invited him in, but what he said, well, it stopped us dead in our tracks."

"Why? What did he say?"

She was quiet for a moment as though reliving the scene in her head.

"Mom..."

She glanced over at me with a strange almost giddy smile.

"He said, 'I've come to see the bairn.' And of course, I didn't know what he meant and was about to invite him in when he said, 'The boy. Your boy, I want you to bring me to him.'"

"Me?" I felt a chill run down my left arm, my fingers tingled.

"Well, we told him to leave or we'd call the police. Ted even threatened him with physical harm. The guy only cackled and dashed back out into the night, and shouted, 'The Hourglass never forgets. Beware he who never sleeps.' or something like that anyway."

"How come I was never told about this?" I said, feeling inexplicable anger course through my veins.

"We thought he was... I don't know, some drunk homeless guy. A crazy man passing through town or something. Someone off his meds. We were so tired back then that I remember joking that you were the one who never sleeps. We never even called the police though I suppose we—"

Tires screeched and horns blared. Something hit us hard, shoving me into the side door and breaking the glass. I felt blood trickling down my face and neck. A hard object pinned my leg between the dash and my seat. Dust filled my lungs, and I began coughing. The next thing I noted was the feeling of weightlessness for a few seconds and then the weight of gravity pulling me into my seat. Metal twisted in horrific squeals.

▲▼▲▼▲

The motion and noise suddenly ceased, or maybe I had blacked out for a moment and then come to. All was quiet. For a few moments, all I could do was inhale shakily. I opened my eyes, slowly at first, until put together what had happened. Trapped inside the car, we'd rolled down an embankment into a roadside ditch. Feeling hazy and nauseous, I tried weakly to push at the door. It groaned as the hinges buckled and snapped. With a final heave, I kicked with my free leg and the door popped off, clanging onto the ground. Cool air flowed in. In the distance I heard the sounds of approaching sirens. Then a voice nearby.

"Is she alive?" It was rough and nasal.

I groaned and attempted to turn my head and glance over. Mom had slumped forward against her seatbelt, hair covered her face. My injuries, albeit painful, seemed only superficial. Feeling had returned to my body, and I reached for my seatbelt clip. A gloved hand appeared in my peripheral.

"This here is a child, Gragchot." This voice was reedier, higher pitched. "We were told she'd be alone. Do we kill the creature?"

Gragchot. Was that a name? *What's going on?*

"We follow orders, filthy scum," the first voice snapped.

"We are to obtain the woman and no one else. Now move it and keep your trap shut, or else there'll be no flesh for supper!"

Flesh for supper...

I squinted in the dust-filled air. The driver's side door was yanked open. I lay motionless as a hot breath tingled the hairs in my ear. I heard rather then saw my mother being pulled from her seat. Feebly, I reached to grab my mom's sweater sleeve.

"He's awake!" A third voice. "Bash his brains out."

"No, wait," I said. "Help, I need—"

I felt a sharp blow to my neck and the world began to darken at an alarming rate. I let out a groan as the darkness enveloped me, sang to me, and nursed me into a quiet slumber.

▲▽▲▽▲

I tried to open my eyes, and a shaft of intense light bombarded them. I blinked rapidly. A man dressed in white spoke with a pretty young woman. They argued in soft murmurs.

"It came from the very top?" the man murmured in hushed tones. "You ask me to place my morals aside for a cause that goes against the code I swore to..."

I let out a groan, and the man stopped talking. When I tried to move, a sharp pain shot through ribs. I gasped for breath and collapsed back down.

"Just take it easy," the man's voice urged reassuringly. "Please rest. You're in good hands. Nurse, go secure some more, uh, of those pain meds."

I raised my head and groaned. The lights had dimmed, and I could see better. I lay on a soft bed. My legs were exposed while the rest of me was covered in a soft green blanket. I suddenly felt nauseous. My breathing became labored and then without warning my back arched, and I began to tremble on the bed. The man leaned over me his hands on my shoulders

"Blast! Stay with us now. Haylee, get down here on the double! We're losing him!"

My peripheral vision was contracting. I was getting lightheaded.

"Where is she?" I moaned. "My mother… Gragchot…"

▴▾▴▾▴

When I awoke again, my whole body was damp with sweat. A woman's calming voice brought me back to my senses.

"Hello, young man, you're finally awake."

I opened my eyes and saw a hazy view of a woman's face, framed with black hair. Her skin was tanned.

"You've been unconscious in a medically induced coma for three days. I'm your personal attendant. My name is Carroll. You wouldn't happen to remember *your* name, would you?"

"My name is Phoenix," I shook the spots away. "My mother. My mother was driving. Where is she? I think someone…"

I realized with alarm that I couldn't remember what had happened.

"Steady," Carroll said. "You haven't eaten solids in days, and you're in no shape to get all worked up. You were the only one found in the car. Authorities are searching for your parents, but so far nothing. You're lucky to be alive."

"She was driving," I said. "My mother, she picked me up from school. Dad was already missing." The words spilled out in a jumbled heap as I tried sorting through my memories. "I need to find them. The Hourglass will kill them if I don't."

"You may have some uncomfortable side effects including confusion. It's common for people in severe vehicle accidents to dream up a fantasy world of fear and paranoia. Voices can seem to be speaking to you. We had to put you on a high dose of pain medication to stabilize you. Dr. Simon prescribed you the dose himself. He's a foremost expert in the field of head trauma."

"You don't understand," I groaned, sitting up as a peppering of pain sprinkled all across my body. "The Hourglass, it's out there, and he or she or it has my parents."

"The Hourglass? After your collision, first responders found you unconscious in the driver's seat," Carroll soothed, lightly pushing on my shoulders in a nurse's way of laying me back down. "Please, do not put any more physical exertion on yourself." She stopped, and a slight frown crossed her face as she began pressing buttons on a console. "You were brought into Emergency and treated immediately. They think you've suffered a serious concussion as well as fractured ribs and possible internal bleeding."

"No that's not right. I was driving it was… I'm leaving." I tried to throw the covers off. The weight of the hospital blankets and my weak limbs made the feat nearly impossible.

Carroll placed a gentle arm on my back, supporting me as I sat. Her motherly care and soft hand brought tears to my eyes. She handed me a glass of transparent liquid. The warm liquid settled into my empty stomach, and before long a welcoming sense of drowsiness enveloped my every thought. The urge to leave began to fade off as the comfortable mattress and warm blankets soothed me. Without warning, I bolted up. Carroll, who had been working at a computer in the next room, dashed in, chattering away about my love of danger.

"Honestly, Phoenix," she grumbled, "you won't be doing anyone any favors, your parents or yourself if you suffer a setback. Now get back in bed."

I was on my feet. How had that happened?

I staggered to the doorway, IV and all. Something was wrong. Both my parents had known about the Hourglass long before Dad had been kidnapped and Mom had found the message in his office. What had Mom said? I stumbled into the hallway. Patients and staff alike looked at me like I was a crazed psychopath. Mom had said something about telling me.

"Phoenix," Carroll's voice cracked from my room, her voice suddenly frigid, "return before I resort to tactics I'd rather not."

Bleary eyed, I turned around. For a split second, a horrid

creature with the head of a spider and the body of a deformed man stood in the doorway. Pounding my fists against my skull, I looked again. The monster was replaced by a furious Carroll. Her eyes glowed with anger. Stomping over, Carroll took me be the arm, directing me back to the room. Her hand was freezing to the touch.

"What is in this medicine you gave me?" I mumbled, feeling my tongue grow three sizes and adopt the fur of a small animal.

"Get into bed," Carroll replied curtly. She pushed her hair out of her face and placed my IV stand next to the bedside. "You will be discharged from the ward by this time tomorrow provided you don't go around giving heart attacks to the staff."

I gave her a befuddled look, as my brain shut down. Eyes heavy with the mysterious drug, I slipped away into an inky blackness, complete with utter isolation.

▲▼▲▼▲

I awoke to Carroll shaking my arm. Her rage-induced demeanor had since been replaced with a calm exterior.

"Wake up sleepyhead," she said softly. "You're going home."

I sat up groggily and rubbed my eyes. The sound of the machines that had, up until this point, been my only companions became quiet. The room was bathed in a warm glow, and the flow of people outside my room had thinned to only staff.

I stood up, brushing the blankets away and glancing down. I gawked at my scrawny, pale legs. I'd clearly lost weight since my admittance into the emergency ward.

"You can dress in the bathroom," Carroll said with a smile. "Mrs. Chase will sign you out. Her documents are in order, but should you feel uncomfortable or ever in danger from anyone while you are in her care, you are more than welcome to return and report her. If you need any help dressing just knock on the door."

I changed into jeans and a polo shirt and slipped my aching

feet back into my faded red sneakers. I let out a sigh of relief at feeling something that was mine. I checked myself in the mirror and noted my scrawny body and frazzled hair. Black splotches had formed under my eyes.

I threw the green robe onto the bed and walked out of the room, closing the door behind me. Carroll showed me the way to the front desk, admiring my choice of shoes in a distant manner. Glancing up, I stopped mid-stride. Katy Chase watched me as I slowly descended the stairs from the second floor, where the patient wing was situated, to the lobby. I felt my face flush as I smiled awkwardly.

"Oh Phoenix dear, how good to see you!" Katy's mom. I hadn't noticed her standing there. "Did they treat you well? I have nothing but confidence in the staff here."

I smiled and embraced Mrs. Chase. The simple act brought a welcome feeling of relief as my pent-up emotions began to melt away. The nurse at the front desk handed Mrs. Chase a clipboard, which she promptly began to fill out.

Carroll offer a dim smile. "It's just a form saying that Mrs. Chase has signed you out of the ward and has adopted the role of guardian until your parents are found."

"How are you feeling, Phoenix?" Mrs. Chase queried in a concerned mother's voice. She handed the clipboard back to Carroll. The nurse turned and ascended the staircase.

"Fine, Mrs. Chase." A lie. "I'm just glad to get out of here. The last several of days have been, well..."

I glanced back and saw Carroll standing at the top of the stairs, watching me. She waved and gave me a big smile. I smiled back. As we turned a corner, her smile abruptly vanished.

"I was simply horrified to hear about your parents," Mrs. Chase began, as she hustled us toward the lobby exit. "I knew then you would need a place to stay so I offered my services. Did you know that last year I took in three foster children?" Of course, I did. I was friends with Katy. "Adorable little chubby bunnies they were but grew out of my ability to care for them.

I'm still registered as a foster mother in the system."

"Thank you, Mrs. Chase. I really appreciate you bringing me into your house all of the sudden like this." Guilt began to form as I realized how much time she had invested into my safety.

She patted my shoulder. "It's the least I could do for you and your parents. This is a distressing time for all."

We arrived at a dusty white minivan. I climbed into the backseat with Katy. The seat was frayed. Katy sat in the spot next to me and gave me a small smile.

"I heard what happened," Katy whispered softly. "I'm so sorry, Phoenix. It seems so strange. I mean I just talked to your mom a couple days ago, and now she's missing? I have a plan for finding your mom and dad. I know this is going to seem unbelievable but hear me out. Do you know Temper?"

I frowned as Mrs. Chase started the car. "Of course, I know him," I said, "or know *of* him at least. The old guy who lives on the end of Larry's block. Katy, he's a known criminal and gang member, or at least that's what he tells anyone who'll listen."

Katy cleared her throat, awkwardly. "Right, but you need to go visit him. I *know* it sounds crazy, but I've been talking to him for a while now, and well, he seems to be in a better place. I talked with him yesterday about what happened, and it seemed to deeply disturb him. He wants to discuss matters with you."

"You want me to go talk about my missing parents to a crazy old man?" I snorted. "Katy, I thought I was the one who was injured."

Trepidation crossed her face, like dark clouds over the sun. Suddenly, I wasn't feeling too comfortable. The smells of gasoline wafted in from the car window. Cars honked, and muffled shouts carried across the pavement as the wind whistled past.

"Katy, look, I appreciate that you're concerned for me, but how is Temper going to be able to help? The guy supposedly has a rap sheet longer than I am tall. What good will visiting him do?"

"Trust me!" Katy gave me a long stare, her eyes pools of determination. Clutching at her seatbelt, she seemed to be willing herself to move forward, as if the act would force me into compliance. "Phoenix, if you never trusted me before, give me this one shot. I know it may seem like a strange move, but the police are not going to be able to help you. Even if they managed to find your parents, it could take years."

"And what if it doesn't?" I snapped back, heat rising to my face. "What if tomorrow my parents are escorted home, and the person responsible for their abduction is cast into the darkest cell imaginable? How do you know what is going to happen? The police and FBI have safely rescued all sort of people before. What's to say this is any different?" I clenched my hands into fists and kneaded the seat fabric.

The car bounced over the gravel road, tiny pebbles smacking the underside of the van like fingers tapping in haunted torment. Katy raised her head and parted her hair so she could see me clearly. Her eyes had become wells of tears. Mrs. Chase, who had up until this point been silent, cleared her throat. We turned to face her.

"If I may interject, Phoenix dear," she said sweetly, her head turned away from us, watching the road. "I don't mean to make a dark matter blacker, but I wouldn't..." -her voice caught- "It's just that my husband vanished when Katy was only three years old. The last time I had seen him he had been furiously scrambling through his desk at home, frantically searching for something. I returned to the kitchen and heard a crash. I rushed back and the room's window had been smashed in and my husband was nowhere to be seen. If you attempt anything dangerous, you yourself may face the same result that your parents are now facing. Let the authorities handle this. It isn't easy sitting back and allowing someone else to have control over how your parents return home, but it is safe and responsible. Don't go rushing into this."

I watched the buildings lumbering by. I waited for Mrs. Chase to continue, but the car remained silent as the three of us withdrew into our respective thoughts. We bounced over a speed bump and drove on leaving a schoolyard behind. We turned off the main road and rumbled down a small street. Mrs. Chase pulled into their driveway, shutting off the engine, and Katy opened her door. I hopped out behind her, feeling satisfied to be at a place of familiarity. The white picket house was set away from the main road. Several tall spruces blocked most of the home from view and the freshly cut lawn gave a relaxing scent of the outdoors. The gravel walkway to the home was wet, as if it had just endured a short rainfall. Bushes and flowers decorated both sides of the path. Flowers with yellows, reds, and greens brought a homey feeling to the abode.

"Promise me, Phoenix," Mrs. Chase said into the uncomfortable silence, "that whatever you do, you do not act rashly. Let the authorities handle this. Katy means well, but you should put your trust in the law because if there is any hope of rescuing your parents, the authorities will handle it."

She walked around the car and unlocked the front door. The house was clean and spacious. I ogled the arched ceilings and spacious rooms. A cat slunk off a burgundy couch and disappeared into a hallway. The walls were laden with paintings and various depictions of the mountains. Wooden floors gave way to carpeted rooms and hanging from the ceiling were several fans.

"You're dead meat!"

A throaty screech from another room. I jumped, feeling a spike of fear, but Katy placed a hand on my shoulder. Her hand brought a sense of comfort. I offered a small smile of gratitude.

"It's just our parrot, Galactic," she said. "We may have taught him some phrases in the past that he, unfortunately, hasn't forgotten." She waited for Mrs. Chase to bustle into the kitchen through an ornate doorway. "The police never found

Dad. If they couldn't find him after these years, I doubt they can find your parents. We never found out what happened to him, but the way my mom doesn't talk about it, it must have been devastating. She still won't tell me everything."

"Gee," I said attempting a smile, "you sure cheered me up."

"I'm trying to appeal to your rational side," she shook her head.

"I just lost both my parents and you think my rational side is what needs to be appealed? Katy, I lost my entire family, I'm alone in this world, and I am terrified. This Hourglass has taken both of my parents! What am I supposed to do against such evil?"

"You're supposed to fight until you find them. You don't back down until they are back with you. I'm sorry I came across as cold. I am trying to help you. Please just visit Temper. He's turned a new leaf, and lately he's had some really good advice. He served overseas, you know. He's seen some pretty gruesome scenes, the kind most of us only see in our worst nightmares. He knows what it is like to lose people he loves. If nothing beneficial comes from this, I will wholeheartedly support you however you want to approach it."

"Why do you want me to talk to him so much?" I asked as we walked into the dining area. "What makes you so sure he can help me? I barely know the guy!"

"Because he helped me," she responded, softly.

"Does your mom know you're talking to him?"

"No," she said and gave me a look that clearly stated I was to say nothing to anyone about this conversation. "I grew up without my dad, and Temper stepped in to fill the role. He may be a bit crazy, but his intentions are good."

I raised my hands in surrender. "Alright, I'll visit him tomorrow. At this point, I'd do just about anything if it meant finding what happened to both of our parents."

Katy smiled, and her cheeks flushed in the dull light filtering through the curtains. She gazed at me for a second.

"Will and Tim are coming over after school to see how you're coping. They've been texting and calling me since you've been in the hospital. I told them you finally were discharged today, and they want to check in on you.

I watched her bustle into the kitchen to help Mrs. Chase with dinner and thought about the day's events. It was all too much to take in. I thought about Temper. I would go and visit him. I prayed I'd come out of all this with more answers than I had questions.

2 ‣ Tempered Step

The shadowed room created the illusion of never-ending darkness. A stooped figure sat on an obsidian throne on a black dais, situated at the center of the cavernous chamber. Around him stood seven figures in billowing black robes. Red hourglass forms decorated the black folds of their rich vestments. Raul stood off to one side and bit the inside of his cheek, nervously. The Hourglass, which was to say the seven hooded forms above, had grown fond of prolonged periods of silence. As Raul continued to watch the eight figures on the dais, a door in the side of the room opened slightly, revealing a disheveled guard. A single sliver of harsh orange light pierced the darkness. Raul squinted.

The guard's head turned from Raul to the man on the throne. He snapped to attention, facing the ominous presence that resided on the dais. The seven robed men retreated into the shadows, whispering in haunting tones to each other. The figure on the throne stirred, becoming aware of the guard's presence.

"The captive has been brought in, my liege," said the guard, a nervous expression crossing his face. "She's been placed on the lower levels."

"What of the boy?" The figure on the throne murmured. His voice was sibilant, slithering into and out of the ears of his terrified men. The seven robed individuals moved silently from the light and faded into the darkness.

"We couldn't obtain him, my Lord Widow." The guard's

demeanor shifted with concern. "He wasn't at the building our operative informed us of."

The Black Widow, the figure on the dais, moved ever so slightly on the throne. He raised his head and revealed two piercing black eyes from beneath his grimy, unkempt hair. The two torches in the chamber revealed the rotten splotches of skin which dotted his face. The pale hue around him was enhanced with the stench of decomposing flesh as his piercing stare drilled into the guard. Lips pale white, he opened his mouth.

"I'm waiting," the Widow hissed. His voice had become deadly soft. Raul twitched with apprehension.

"We were told he would be in class. Our operative was able to enter the building of education and personally identity the boy. We waited for him to leave for the day, but he never departed. We successfully retrieved the women from her vehicle wreckage. Gragchot did mention that he found a young boy in the car but left him behind." At his last words, the guard's eyes widened in horror as he realized what he'd just uttered. His face drained of color and his mouth opened wordlessly.

"Please, my lord," he finally collapsed to his knees, "don't order me to the Pit!"

"Raul?" the Widow murmured. His hair fell once more over his lifeless eyes. "See to it that this guard is made an example of those who fail me."

Raul glanced at the sobbing guard, who had dropped all pretense of professionalism and openly begged for his life.

"My liege," Raul began, "perhaps a demotion would serve him better? We are running low on men and Shades as it is and..."

The Widow turned to look at Raul, and for a moment, Raul felt a cold pain erupt in his chest as the flesh above his heart began to bubble and the feeling of something inside him sent spasms of twitches through his body. Raul hastily beckoned for a guard to remove the other. The sobbing guard was led away. Raul could sense their fear.

"Raul?" the Widow called.

"My lord?" Raul cleared his throat, carefully avoiding looking directly into the man's penetrating stare.

"My plan cannot come to fruition without the boy." The voice echoed through the space, bouncing off of the stone walls and colliding in unnerving rhythm. "Gragchot failed us."

"We have located him, my lord." Raul fixed his collar carefully, noting the sweat that now coated his body. "One of our operatives reported back that the boy was discharged from the hospital and now abides with the Chases. I have one of our last horde of Shades ready for your command."

The Widow's eyes shimmered, and the once lifeless black became fiery red as he stood and extended his arms. "I've trusted you this far and allowed you my full resources and powers over my creations. Do not fail me now, or your fate will be far worse than any you've yet witnessed. The boy must be brought to me."

Raul felt the sweat trickle down his side, sticking his suit to his skin.

"Furthermore, my lord, our operative has informed us that the boy has been convinced to consult the Old One."

For a moment Raul was afraid he'd advanced too far. A mist had begun to float around the ceiling and the temperature dropped. The darkness grew thicker, like a wall of blackness. The Widow descended the dais, his back to Raul.

"Fifty years…" the Widow said softly, placing his fingers to his temple. "Fifty years I've waited in this shamble of a hideout. Fifty years I've waited to be free. The boy must be convinced to set out and find his family. I do not need to inform you what will happen should this plan fail?"

Raul shivered violently as he bowed his head. He had seen many of his former operatives in this position, frozen under the gaze of his master. Many times over, he'd seen this same threat laid against them.

"I will redouble my efforts." Raul knelt, quaking. "My best agents will be sent out to ensure the trap is laid to a perfection worthy of your approval. I will not fail you, my Lord Widow! Our operative in his inner circle has reported back. Were the very hands of Ëonë poised to smite down from above, I would die before I failed you."

▲▼▲▼▲

I stood on the porch of the Chase home as the night yielded to pale rays of dawn. Four more days had passed since I'd been released from the hospital. Katy stood by my side, and I glanced apprehensively at her. Her body was rigid, her posture showing her unease. She turned and even before she spoke, I knew what she would say.

"I'm coming! I'm coming with you to see Temper!"

I looked up at the Blue Bear, a landmark which loomed in the distance. The body was fashioned as a bear on its hind legs, readying to swipe at its meal. Composed of dog tags, the bear commemorated two hundred thousand citizens of the state of Colorado who had given their lives in the line of duty. Above the statue, a jet aircraft rumbled overhead. The green painted engines reflected the dull sunlight. A soft breeze had started and played with the lose strands of her hair. I breathed deeply.

"It could be dangerous," I murmured as we watched the sunrise. The red ball of light crested the horizon. "Even if Temper can help, I don't know if I'm able to face my fears. The Hourglass kidnapped my mom and presumably my dad. What can an old man and I do against that?"

"It isn't a worthless mission," she said as she gazed out across the street. "I know this helplessness you're going through. Losing a loved one, especially one who is so close to you, is painful. I know you're willing to accept any avenue that might lead to an end to this pain. Let me provide that avenue. Besides, it won't just be you and Temper. I'm coming along too, remember?"

She nudged me with her shoulder, and I leaked a small grin.

The sun rose higher, and even the darkest shadows fled before its harsh light. There was something comforting about standing on the porch with Katy.

"I know." My voice cracked. "I feel desperate. I've never felt so alone before."

Katy placed her hand on mine and intertwined her fingers with my own. I gazed out at the mountains before us. The actions of the previous week had been trying on not just myself, but Katy and her mom. Both were so willing and happy to care for me, but deep inside it was taking a toll on both. My depression and bouts of deep thinking had begun to unnerve them.

"Phoenix, Katy, dear? Breakfast is ready. You mustn't let the coffee cool down. I made some of my special bacon-and-egg salad!"

Katy's mom hovered at the open sliding door, doing her best to appear upbeat.

"Your bacon-and-egg salad is irresistible, Mrs. Chase," I admitted, letting my hand go from Katy's. "I'm coming! By the way, is it okay if I head out for a bit later this morning? Also, it would really help me if Katy came with me?"

Mrs. Chase's eyes fogged over, her shaky smile wavering. "Oh, whatever for? I don't think you should be out and about just yet. The events of the past week can be trying on you. It would be better to stay home, eat up, and rest."

I glanced hesitantly at Katy, but she leaned against the railing and stared off toward the looming peaks of the Rocky Mountains. The dark heaps of rock and soil stood ominously. I turned back to Mrs. Chase, who was waiting expectantly.

"I'm going to visit a friend who might be able to help me."

Heat coursed through my cheeks and I felt the urge to look away, rub my neck, or do anything but look Mrs. Chase in the eye. The statement, while not a lie, was not an entire truth, and even the thought of lying to Mrs. Chase after her hospitality made my throat close up.

"Katy?" Mrs. Chase cleared her throat.

"We're just going visit a friend." Katy nodded. "It'll be some much-needed therapy for Phoenix. Trust me, Mom. I'll make sure he is okay and comes home."

Mrs. Chase gave one final look at me before nodding, wordlessly. We slipped past her into the dining room and took our seats at the oaken table. Food was displayed appetizingly along a back counter as plates were set at each of the four chairs. I glanced questioningly up at Mrs. Chase.

"Is someone else coming?" I asked, taking a helping of steaming bacon-and-egg salad. The odors wafted up and my stomach growled appreciatively.

"Oh," she chuckled, throwing some pans into the sink, "I forgot to tell you, Mrs. Gree is dropping Will off. Will said he wanted to visit with the two of you, and I offered him a spot at my table. Hearing that, he couldn't refuse." Her eyes twinkled.

Tires crunching over gravel heralded the arrival of a visitor, and we fell silent. The doorbell rang with the enthusiasm of an eager and hungry guest. Through the windows next to the door, I recognized Will's bright blue shirt. Mrs. Chase bustled forward and opened it, a wide grin on her face. Will waved.

"I couldn't resist your salad, Mrs. Chase." Will grinned as he stepped forward. "And of course, it might be nice to see Phoenix." He caught sight of me, and his grin faltered. He met my eyes.

Katy hurried forward and gave him a hug.

"Hey, Phoenix," Will said into the silence. "How are you? Katy brought me up to speed on the crucial areas."

"Life has been better," I admitted as he seated himself.

"Any major developments on your parents' case?" Will asked as he stuffed his mouth with eggs.

"No," I shook my head and pushed my food around with my fork. "Deputy Chade called yesterday to say all of their leads have gone cold and they have no investigative path to follow for the time being."

Mrs. Chase hurried out of the room and began to hum to

herself as she cleaned dishes in the kitchen. I leaned forward, conspiratorially.

"Katy and I are going to talk to Temper. Katy seems to think he will be able to help me in some fashion."

Will leaned forward and cast a glance back over his shoulder. "I talked to Tim who talked to a neighborhood bloke who lives next to Temper. The kid claims that Temper recently had a visitor. A man dressed in grey. He told Temper to quote 'expect the one we've been waiting for'."

The food sunk like concrete to the bottom of my stomach. I twitched in my seat.

"Like the guy from school? The one in the cafeteria?" I asked.

"Who knows?" Will shrugged. "What are the odds of you heading out to talk to Temper mere hours after some man in grey is seen? The day your mom disappears, a man dressed very similarly shows up—it can't be a coincidence."

"And you think this guy is after me?" I sounded skeptical.

Will shrugged.

"Honestly," Katy interrupted, unusually cold, "how do we even know the man in grey has any relations to what's going on? He could be the mailman telling Temper his long-awaited package is arriving soon."

"A mailman in unprofessional attire that screams 'I am a bad guy'?" Will raised one eyebrow.

Katy shook her head. "The point is coincidences *do* happen on occasion and so does bad hearing. Phoenix, you shouldn't let this deter you! The margin for misinterpreting this series of events is high. Temper is a good guy. I vouch for him. You trust me, right?"

I stirred the eggs into the bacon, watching my fork mix the greasy goodness with the fluffy eggs. My stomach tossed in uncomfortable summersaults. To look at it from an outsider's perspective, I was about to take my friends to a rumored convict's home where, just hours previously, a friend of Will's had seen Temper talking with an enigmatic man warning him to expect someone. A week prior, a man in black had shown up at my school, and less than an hour later, my mom had been kidnapped. Why was it that I felt I should still go? Was it to appease Katy? Or was there some part of me that still clung to the hope that both my parents were still alive and that any answer, however improbable, became the probable?

"I'm going," I decided, placing my fork down. "If there is any chance Temper can help, I don't think I should risk leaving it. We will need to be on heightened awareness."

"And if it turns out that this guy is dangerous and dealing with the people who kidnapped your parents?" Will asked.

"I'll have *you* with me." I turned to Katy.

"My mom has agreed to drive us to Temper's house," Will stated, reluctantly. "Dad didn't need the car, so she's able to spend the day helping you out, Phoenix."

"*You're* coming now?" Katy tilted her head. I glanced between the two of them.

"You seriously think I'd let my best friend go into a potentially harmful situation without real backup?" Will scoffed.

"Harmful situation?" I grimaced. "You make it sound like I'm about to go off and fight in a war." We stood from the table.

I thanked Mrs. Chase for the hearty breakfast and proceeded to follow the group out onto the front porch.

"Does it look a little dark to you?" Katy asked. "This can't be a good omen." Her hair whipped about in the growing wind. Above the mountains, dark clouds clustered. The grey sight brought chills to my spine.

"We're overdue for our next snowfall," I said, feeling my stomach settle uneasily. "I'm sure it is nothing more than that."

Mrs. Gree was parked on the road next to the house and hurried out and opened the sliding van door for us. Will climbed in first, allowing Katy and I to occupy the two middle seats. Mrs. Gree pulled out of the driveway and sped down the main access road.

Time passed quickly. I spent it gazing out of the window. The industrial and business areas gave way to dilapidated homes. The homes lacked color, their once brightly coated walls were left to peel and fade. The yards steadily shrank in size, pavement and rocks becoming more prominent. Trees changed from flourishing spruces to twisted ancient oaks.

"You sure this is safe?" I murmured. "I feel like we aren't in Kansas anymore."

Mrs. Gree pulled the van to a halt, outside a rundown home. The walls had been infected by termites and the wood eaten back to reveal support beams and piping. The paint had long since faded, leaving the house a rusted brown color. The roof had collapsed on one end. Yellow caution tape ran the boundary of the property. Tangled weeds and coarse grass rendered the front yard's unkept appearance.

Mrs. Gree gawked. "Surely you're not going into that home. The place is clearly abandoned. No one could live there."

"This is the address," Will checked his phone. "We'll be right back."

The three of us disembarked from the safety of the van, once again feeling the chill of early winter piercing through our protective clothing.

"Your mom is just letting us walk up to this piece of junk?" Katy marveled, holding her arms close to her body.

"Hold on," Will said, "Phoenix told me you'd been here many times! What makes it different now?"

"For one, the appearance," Katy replied. "Last time I was here there was a functioning roof. Your friend didn't happen to mention what happened to this place did he, Will?"

We hesitantly climbed the front walkway. The cloudy sky and bitter wind added to an atmosphere of intimidation.

Katy took a step forward, knocking lightly on the wooden door. It was the only piece of the house that didn't seem to be suffering from severe termite disorder. No sound or reply echoed from the inside of the house. The silence dragged on. All was quiet.

"He must not be home," I turned away. The lock on the inside of the door clicked. The door was thrown open violently, and standing in the doorway, looking for all intents and purposes like the next heavy-weight champion, was Temper. His biceps and tanned body were only the beginning of our surprise.

"Do you plan to rob me?" He mused, rubbing his thick beard. "Perhaps a local prank brought on through the encouragement of your peers?" Then he caught sight of her. "Katy, is that you? I haven't seen you in a while."

"Hi Temper," she said. "This is Phoenix and Will, two of my friends."

"What brings you to this particularly nasty part of town?" Temper narrowed his eyes and glanced down both ends of the street. "This isn't a safe place for children to be."

"You may have heard about the disappearance of Ted and Ashley Rather," I began. "They were abducted and—"

"You're the boy?" Temper interrupted, his brow furrowing. He stared intently at me.

"I'm Phoenix Rather, their son," I said. "How did you know that? I never..."

But I couldn't finish the thought. Something about the way he was looking at me unsettled me. For a few lengthy moments, Temper said nothing. His eyes seemed to drill into me.

"So you're Phoenix Rather?" His voice dropped an octave—his nostrils flared. "*The* Phoenix Rather?"

For a moment, an unfamiliar emotion crossed his eyes and he coughed to cover it up. He glanced awkwardly at Katy, and my eyes widened in surprise. This escapade had been fraught with holes from the onset, and it appeared we could gain nothing from it.

"Phoenix?" Temper repeated. "Yes, I have heard of you, although I never thought you'd one day be standing on my doorstep. Forgive me, old age has a way of eliminating useful information. Please, do come in. The house, despite its condition, is much warmer than this weather."

We stepped over the threshold, entering a dim hallway. Temper clicked the lock behind us. The finality of the sound sent goosebumps down my arms. Temper escorted us through the hallway into a space where a roaring fire lit the entire room in comforting glow.

"I realize the accommodations may lack a certain pleasantry that we, as social beings, have constructed as the norm." Temper cleared his throat. "The power has been off for several months now. I get by with the occasional candle and good log when I can find one. Phoenix, won't you tell me more about this kidnapping?"

I detailed the entire first day's traumatic events. Temper sat, fully engrossed, glancing away from me only when a shriek of wind shook the house. When I arrived at the letter from the Hourglass, his eyes widened, and he stood.

"The Hourglass?" Temper rubbed his facial hair frantically. "You must be mistaken. They were forcibly disbanded centuries ago." He glanced uneasily out the closest window.

"They are responsible for kidnapping my parents," I said.

"If what you say is indeed true, and the Hourglass is behind this, then the gravity of the situation has shifted. The Hourglass is a group of beings with pure evil as their driving force. They worship and serve one who's name I shall not utter here. Names have power." Temper squinted at us. "You will fail miserably and die knowing you failed. If you seek this path, grief and pain will be your only victories."

"So what am I to do?" I snapped, launching up from where I'd taken a seat. "My parents are out there, maybe still alive, possibly being tortured as we speak. I can't just sit back, relax, and not think about it." I blinked rapidly. The helplessness that had plagued me of late grew to a staggering weight and gushed out. "I'm going to find them. If you aren't willing to help, then I will do it without you."

The room was silent. Will had his head down, his arms folded over his knees as he sat in one corner. Katy, a hand to her mouth, glanced repeatedly between Temper and I. Temper, buff man that he was, seemed to have melted into a fragile body. His arms hung limp at his sides, his mouth contorted into a grimace.

"You youth cast aside the very help you request," he rumbled. "When faced with a formidable adversary, you leap with both feet into the roaring fire without realizing the danger and then blame others for the pain the fire produces. Had I given you positive outcomes, you would have left my presence, confident in my vote of approval and walked straight into evil you couldn't possibly imagine. When you stare death in the face, pain on all sides, what will you think of me then? Will you curse my name? Will you relish the thought of my cursed existence as the life leaves your eyes?" His voice rose to a terrifying rumble as he rose to his feet, hands clenched into monstrous fists. "Would you risk your own precious life for this, Phoenix Rather? Will you be able to accept death in exchange for their life?"

"Stop it!" Katy cried, leaping up and standing between us.

My body quivered with rage, blind tears stinging my eyes. The heat in my face embarrassed me.

"Stop," she said. "Both of you!"

"I would die to save my parents," I said. "My life means nothing to me if it can be used to save others. I would gladly look death in the face if it meant my family could become whole once more."

Temper sat back down, a smile on his face. He crossed both arms and gave me an appraising look.

"Then I shall assist you in your quest," he said. "I see now you value the lives of others more so than your own. This trait is rare. Should you be captured trying to find your parents, you will most certainly die alongside those with you. I can help you, but I cannot promise success, not against the foe you are doomed to face. I am not responsible for what happens to you after. I know of a place where your foe dwells in hiding. You shall visit there and find the location you seek. Aye, I shall help you. But a time will come when you wish I had rejected your plea and had let you live out your life here."

His words, foreboding as they were, brought a sense of purpose back, and I silently thanked him.

The room grew silent again, no one wanting to ruin the moment. Temper gazed at me, his fingertips on the bridge of his nose. Katy seems to have frozen in time, unable to move as she watched the debate unfold.

"I will help you, as far as Pikes Peak." Temper cleared his throat. "The Hourglass will be searching for you, of that much I am sure. An old prophecy is unfolding before my eyes, and I fear I know how it ends. Creatures of the Hourglass have been seen roaming throughout the hills. Their master is on the hunt. You think the Hourglass is the only enemy you are to fear?" He chuckled softly as we all hung in anticipation over his next words. "There is one greater still, one who is embodiment of evil and who, in darkness, created the Hourglass to hunt all who could oppose him."

"How do you know this?" Will asked.

Temper breathed deeply before responding. "Long, long ago in my youth, I faced their master. He is called the Black Widow, a shadowy figure who haunts the thoughts of all who see him. His very image burns through the minds of his enemies until, in pure terror, they submit their will to him. If the Hourglass is indeed the force behind your parents' kidnapping, then he is too."

▲▼▲▼▲

Mrs. Gree, it turned out, had stopped at a donut shop. As we climbed back into the car, she handed back two boxes of glazed donuts. Will grabbed one, consuming it in two bites.

"How was the meeting?" Mrs. Gree asked, cheerfully. Her

driving skills ensured we had minimum disturbance from the multitude of potholes which scattered across the poorly managed road.

"Pikes Peak is one of Colorado's fourteeners." Will said, his mouth half full of donut. "It was originally called El Capitán by the Spanish settlers but was renamed to Pikes Peak after Zebulon Pike Jr. in 1806."

"Excuse me?" Mrs. Gree inquired inquisitively. "Pikes Peak?"

"It's a long story, Mrs. Gree," I said, giving Will a cold look. "We talked with Temper about a couple of things, and he mentioned Pikes Peak. We're trying to figure out its importance. Would you mind taking us to the library? I hate asking this of you, especially after you've been so kind in driving us here."

"Nonsense," she said. "I wouldn't mind it at all."

The library was massive. Two marble lions guarded the gold-plated doors—their stone bodies sculpted in attack postures, open maws and slashing claws. Their flowing manes and piercing eyes guarded the well of knowledge inside.

We hurried up the brick path to the front doors, climbing the wide steps, past an empty stone basin, and shoved open the heavy doors. They swung open, creaking ominously. The inside of the library itself outshone even the most impressive political building. Huge floor to ceiling windows were placed so patrons could sit and enjoy the blue lake behind the building. Shelves of books vanished into the darkness of the ceiling. The walls were covered in colorful mosaics, scenes of the most famous historic events. Napoleon marched his troops across the south wall, giving an unknown command. George Washington breathed into his hands at Valley Forge on the east wall. The western wall seemed to glow with the face of Eve, her flowing hair covering her upper torso. The north wall was blank, but for the scribblings in text of recounts from those who had lived through many wars of the early 19th century. The library was a gem amongst the slowly declining economy in Clearview. In the middle of the room, a sturdy table held several coffee pots. They filled the giant room with the wonderful odor of freshly pressed coffee beans. Pastries were covered in a silky cloth on the table.

"I could come here a hundred times and still be in awe," Katy murmured, eyes wide.

"Welcome to the great library of Clearview!" Will declared, swinging his arms out. "Answers to our questions and food for our starvation of knowledge abide in here."

Stacks of books lined one side of the room, all on small brown tables. A door led to a second room all filled with more books. The librarian, a young woman, sat at her desk. She stared intently at a computer. Her sweater was held tightly around her body, and her short brown hair was stuck in a tight ponytail. She glanced up. I immediately froze. The hair on the back of my neck stood erect. The librarian's eyes were pure black orbs. She smiled.

"Guys," I stammered, feeling a cold spreading through my limbs, "do you see that?"

Behind me, Katy's mouth was open, her eyes glued to the figure before us. Will had dropped the book he had been holding and swallowed.

"Run!" A deep voice roared.

The voice was all I needed to clear my head. I whirled about and watched as Temper flung the library doors open. We frantically fled toward him. The sounds of snarling and snapping came from behind us. The librarian, or whatever she was, had climbed over the desk and was running for us. She now held a gleaming sword in her hands. Temper gestured frantically as we barreled through the opening, out onto the front patio. I tripped on a shoelace, tumbling down the steps and crashing into the empty basin. Blood trickled down the back of my head and spots danced across my vision. My hearing dulled to far-off cries and the sounds of the doors being slammed. Someone grabbed my arm, hoisting me up.

"I can't…" I tried, mumbling thickly.

My vision cleared enough for me to see Temper leaning his full weight against the library doors, which shuddered as the librarian slammed herself against them. Mrs. Gree hurried and opened the car door. The book she'd been reading fell to the cement as she hustled the three of us in.

"Phoenix," she asked, "whatever happened? Oh my, you're bleeding! Sit down. I think I have a first aid kit in the trunk."

"No time!" Will cried. Outside, Temper had abandoned his post and hurried toward us. The doors splintered open, buckling under the pressure of some unseen force. A form, hooded and robed, issued forth, a single broadsword held in one hand. No discernible features could be seen save for two glistening orbs of light where eyes normally sat. Lifting its head, the form made a horrible screech and dashed toward us. It had inhumane speed and closed the distance between us rapidly.

"Temper!" I yelled. "Temper behind you!"

He whirled around, and the hooded form stopped, mere feet from him. For a brief moment they stared at each other. In one fluid movement, the form slashed its sword and rushed forward. Temper, ducking, caught the tip of the blade and cried out as he fell. The thud of his body against the concrete rang in my ears and I leapt forward. The form moved to send the blade into my chest. I raised my arms. Temper bellowed and collided with it. Mrs. Gree, her eyes wide with horror, dashed to the driver's door, yanking it open and jamming the key into the ignition. Temper, having fended off the form, slammed his meaty fist against the glass of the car's window.

"Let him in!" I cried, feeling a frantic tension build up as the black creature stalked forward. "He's a friend, that's Temper. Let him in, please!"

The door unlocked, Temper staggered in, holding his side and gesturing wildly with his free hand.

"Get us out of here!" he rasped, wincing.

Mrs. Gree needed no further encouragement as she stomped

the gas pedal and screeched out of the parking space.

As we sped away, I turned in the backseat, watching. The figure never attempted to follow, instead it watched as we sped away.

"What was that thing?" I asked.

"It's a servant of the enemy," Temper groaned and clamped the cloth Mrs. Gree had supplied against his side. "You can't afford to wait until tomorrow anymore. You need to leave tonight. It's not safe here. The Widow already has his shades looking for you. I was mistaken to wait so long. Events are now in motion that have slipped from my control!"

"Am I supposed to not listen?" Mrs. Gree snapped. "What are you telling these kids? Leave where? Will certainly isn't leaving anywhere, not after curfew. Class is tomorrow, and he has not finished any of his homework."

"Creatures have descended from the hills," Temper said, grimacing again as blood began to appear through the cloth. "None of us are safe while that thing knows what we look like. It came for your four and now it knows I reside here. I can promise you it will search and search until it finds you, and one day you will not awake from your deep slumber. It is the only way."

"Will?" Mrs. Gree demanded hotly.

"We'll talk about this later, Mom," Will responded. He glanced apprehensively at me, clutching his seatbelt hard enough to turn his fingers white. "We'll talk about this later, I promise!"

We drove in silence. The morning had turned into later afternoon and the sun had begun its descent. Snowflakes fell and the wind began to increase in ferocity. As we neared the Chase homestead, Katy finally spoke.

"Temper's right." Will and I glanced at her. "Whatever that thing was, it clearly intended to maim or worse kill us. Phoenix, I know that you feel you are asking a lot from us to help you, especially after that thing attacked us. We are with you, however, or at least I am."

She glanced at Will.

"You're voting we abandon our families and continue with Phoenix?" Will asked.

"No," I said. "I am going on alone to find out what happened, and you both are returning home, where it's safe."

"We won't be safe!" Katy argued. "Didn't you hear Temper? That thing at the library saw all four of us. It knows what we look like and he knows we are your friends. None of us are safe. If we return home and act like nothing happened, we'll have it on our doorsteps within a few days. This is the perfect chance to head out with you and find your parents."

"It would just go after our own parents," Will murmured, his voice had dropped to a slight whisper. "We don't even know that that thing had anything to do with Phoenix's parents' disappearance."

"Yes," I snorted, "because a sword wielding spider thing in a library trying to kill people is completely normal and an everyday occurrence."

"I'm not saying that that thing wasn't trying to harm us," Will said. He stared helplessly at me, unable to form the rest of his thought.

"So what would you suggest?" Katy asked. "If we aren't safe at home, and there are things hunting us, what would you recommend?"

"We go with Phoenix on his quest," Will concluded. "I'm here to see this through the end. This is no game. That thing made it evident that they will not hesitate to kill us. The road will be fraught with dangers and possible death."

I shook my head. "I can't ask you to come with me. It'll be too dangerous. Temper and I will continue."

"You don't have the authority to *prevent* us from joining with you." Will gave me a small smile. "I am here to help and to see this through to the end. When Temper awakes, we can discuss this more."

As Will and Katy bickered, I brooded. The creature had very

clearly been waiting for us at the library. I hadn't even planned on visiting the library until after I'd talked with Temper. The creature had mobilized and set up a trap before I'd even really known where we were headed. If we left on this journey to save my parents, as both Temper and I had planned, the Grees and Chases respectively would be hunted down until the creature had gained all the information it could handle. If the parents knew of our plans it would only put them in danger. I knew of only one outcome, one exit, one plan. I leaned forward, clearing my throat so as to catch Will and Katy's attention. I whispered underneath the rumbles of the car's engine.

"The only way we can be sure to protect our families is to give as little information as possible. I'm ready to leave as soon as night falls. Plan accordingly but don't bring much. We need to be light and able to move quickly. I don't ask either of you to risk your lives for this. I can't ask that. But I can't stop you. Pikes Peak is our best hope for a lead on the Widow's location, and Temper and I will head for it at nightfall. If you still want to come, we'll meet outside the abandoned batting cages on the northside of town. I'd wait till morning, but every moment we wait is another risk. I won't waste a moment more. Are you with me?"

"I'm with you," Will nodded solemnly. "I pledge my life to you, Phoenix. I will be with you through pain and joy should both come to me."

"You have my trust and loyalty and well." Katy gripped my hand. "Whatever happens, I am by your side. Through life and death, we will follow you until we bring your parents home."

▲▼▲▼▲

Nighttime fell and Katy and I met Temper outside the abandoned batting cages. A wind had rustled up and sent snow whirling through the air. I hugged my jacket to my body and kicked at the powdering of snow that had begun to accumulate. Temper, eyes glued to the mountains, breathed steadily. His breath ballooned and his nose reddened. I glanced up as footsteps over gravel caught my attention. I smiled as Will stepped beneath the light of a small streetlamp. My smile faltered when I saw who stood beside him.

"Tim?" A bad feeling welled up in my stomach. "Tim, I'm not asking you to come with us. Will, well he wasn't supposed to... this was not part of the deal."

"You honestly believe I'd stay behind?" Tim blew into his hands. His dreadlocks, once brown in color, now bore the white of winter. He clapped his hand on my shoulder. "I may not have seen this character you guys are up in arms about, but I know well enough to see that you guys are in true danger. Will has given me the skinny on things so I know the risks and made the choice to come."

"Will?" I raised one eyebrow as he ducked his head.

"Tim and I started talking, and before I knew it, it all came out."

"How many people *did* you tell?" I sounded peevish. "Maybe we should make a Facebook page so people could line the road and cheer as we head off?"

"Don't be so harsh," Katy stood at my side. She'd dressed preparedly, heavy pants with a thick coat. Her beautiful hair was hidden beneath a cap which hugged the tips of her ears. "I told him too, though after Will did, and he's truly dedicated to coming with us. He's your friend, Phoenix. You can't turn him away."

"I was meant to do this alone." But was that true? It didn't matter; that's how it felt. "And now I've now I've dragged you three along. If anything happens to any of you... I mean, I care for you all and I do not want to see you hurt."

I turned and looked out toward the mountains. Black peaks capped with faint white blankets seemed infinitely far away. The grey clouds above seems to close down around us. The potential dangers seemed all too real and all too deadly. Just a few weeks ago, I'd been a normal teenager in the dog days of summer with another school year ahead of him.

"Hey man, we're all grownups." Tim smiled. "Besides, like Katy said, you have no choice. I'm coming with you, Phoenix Rather, if it's the last thing I do."

"I think we've all sealed our own fates." Will said this like a joke, but it didn't land properly and failed to lighten the mood.

"Hush!" Temper's strained voice silenced our conversation and we turned. From the darkness of the night, the whinny of horses. A figure dressed in grey emerged from the side of the road, holding the reigns to five horses. The man's eyes seemed to glow in the light from the lamp.

"We move out!" Temper ordered and I slung the small sack I'd brought over my shoulder. The cans of dried vegetables and beans clinked together. Will and Tim were similarly equipped, sporting rugged knapsacks. Only Katy seemed to have prepared for the potential danger. Her backpack, although large, was light enough for her to carry with ease.

"I've gone and secured mounts," Temper growled, shifting his hat low. "Take only what you need. If you have difficulties riding horseback, prepare to learn quickly. We ride with the shadows of the east to our backs!"

I felt my spirits rise as the six horses cantered to a stop before us.

The grey clad figured bobbed his head in greeting. "Temper, these are the mounts you bade me to bring. The pack horse is stocked with enough provisions to last you several weeks alone. Will you not allow my men and I to travel with you? The mountain has become a hornet's nest of activity. Shades have been spotted farther east than before. The Widow is making his move."

"Nay, Thornburg my friend," Temper said. "You have done more than the tales will ever tell. Be at peace should I fail. Look for me on the eve of the equinox, a fortnight's time from now. I shall return, or not, by then. Hold your men ready to ride. It is imperative that we complete this mission, but too many in our company will draw attention. Secrecy is our ally now."

Thornburg bowed slightly and in a few brief moments, vanished into a thicket of trees. His sudden arrival and departure filled me with unease. I rubbed my stomach.

"Anyone else getting really creepy vibes from this?" Tim muttered. "I mean I was able to watch *Cabin in the Woods* without covering my eyes but now..."

"Fear not, Timothy," Temper murmured, his face turned toward the narrow dirt path we would take. "All things will be explained in due course. For now, save your energy and be silent. The road is long and evil stirs under the blanket of night. Keep up your courage."

I heaved myself onto the back of a massive stallion whose mane flowed in the soft breeze. His black coat and speckled face made me think of stars in the night sky.

"Phoenix," Temper said as he mounted his own horse, "you ride upon the noble Athillion. Katy, you will be carried by the young Ultumno. Will, Finniwen shall carry you. He's the brown horse near the back. Timothy, over there the milky white horse shall be your steed. His name is Glas. These four steeds have been specially trained for this type of arduous journey. Worry not for them. The small one at the very back is Whipper, our pack horse. He is the son of Ultumno, and a fine steed indeed."

Tim and Will mounted up, Will needing a hand to get into the saddle. Katy tied the packs to Whipper and then mounted Ultumno, Temper leaned forward to his horse, and it dawned on me that he had not shared its name.

"Ride," he whispered in the beast's ear. "Take us to the halls of hell! Fear not the spears which would jab at you. When I ride upon you, you shall know no fear!"

3 · First Blood

The sun had crested the mountains and the snow let up before Temper allowed us to rest. We'd ridden tirelessly through the early hours of the morning without stopping. The path Temper guided us along was invisible to our eyes, yet Temper assured us he followed a trail known only to him. By the time the thin layer of snow had begun to melt, we'd come to a halt. All around a serene backdrop of natural peace hung silently. The clear mountain air gripped my lungs. A soft wind played through the treetops and tickled at our already cold faces. My ears were red with cold and I rubbed them. The tips of my fingers felt useless despite the gloves Temper had given me. The soft animal fur lining had since been unable to prevent the cold. The coat I'd worn wanted for a scarf and the morning air worked itself beneath the collar. I shivered. For all its beauty and majesty, I preferred the mountains at a distance and the cold even further.

"Get Whipper, Katy," Temper ordered as he swung off his steed. We'd arrived in a clearing. "My companions will have prepared a breakfast for us, if you can call it that." He rubbed his arms as the chilly wind carried the morning along. "There are blankets as well in the packs. Do not get too comfortable for we cannot rest long. Every mile we ride brings us closer to the Widow, and he won't want that."

I wearily slipped off of Athillion, patting his strong flank before staggering to a fallen tree. My inner thighs burned with a painful fire. Will walked over as he munched on a granola bar.

His face was all but buried in the heavy jacket he'd brought. Katy rummaged through our packs. Since we'd left Clearview at our backs, she'd remained silent. I watched her as she brought out the beginnings of a promising meal.

"What do you think so far?" Tim winced. "As far as running away from normal life and facing down an evil force goes, I think it's turning out pretty swell."

I rubbed my inner thighs. The wind changed abruptly, and a branch full of snow cascaded around my head. I cried out and slapped at the fallen snow. It had slipped inside my jacket and I began to shiver uncontrollably. Katy, her eyes pools of concern, rushed over and assisted. When I began to feel the comfort of warmth again, she returned to her work.

"Temper is taking us on a more or less straight path to Pikes Peak. I don't expect it'll take us more than a day if the horses keep this pace," Will said. "As to leaving normal life, I am glad, though I grieve the reason we left. While Clearview suffocated me with its uneventful existence, it was still home. Thoughts of traveling and engaging in conflict for a cause, while noble, has caused me not a small amount of concern. I pray I may be found useful before the end, whatever end that may be."

"Gosh," I said, "you can't be super depressing already. We have yet to confront and fight our enemy."

"Have you already forgotten the demon spawn at the library?" Will stared at me. In a cold turn, his voice had grown sharper. "That thing nearly ended all of us. We chose to come since staying behind meant death. I pledged my loyalty to this quest because I see it as the only possible way to survive. I want all of us to survive. Our enemy is very real, and we've already seen what power lies against us. Even Temper barely fended them off—no offense intended of course."

Temper inclined his head as he sipped from a cup.

"I don't mean to underplay the dangers we are in," I said, speaking softly now. "I'm as aware as any of us of dangers this quest may pose. My parents are living, I hope, proof of the evil we fight against. If there is any chance of saving them, I have to try. Temper, tell us what we're up against."

"Nightshades have been seen east of us but a half day's ride. The man we spoke with prior to leaving has kept me informed, and from what I know, it isn't pretty. We surprised them by our sudden flight to the mountains, but they now know our intent." Temper's voice was firm, yet I couldn't help but notice the cup shaking in his hand, its contents sloshing around.

"You still haven't really told us what nightshades are," Will said, popping the last bit of his bar into his mouth. "Are they hired mercenaries? Terrorists?"

"All would be better alternatives to what we face." Temper grimly shook his head. "No, nightshades are a twisted race of creatures, born in the dark of a time long passed. They travel by shadow. Their bodies are human to all appearances save for their heads."

"Travel by shadow?" Katy said, walking up with an armful of blankets. "How does someone travel by shadow? Do you mean at night?"

"I fear our short rest is almost up and that tale would take more time to tell than we have at our disposal." Temper smiled. He accepted a soft blanket and wrapped it around his wide shoulders. "The nightshades' heads are massive arachnid skulls, complete with eight eyes and pinchers deadly enough to decapitate someone. When they are out here in the world of men, they wear hoods and sunglasses to cover their less humanlike appearances. Their pinchers can retract into the flesh of their jaw, and their eight eyes can morph into two, leaving for all intents and purposes a human face—provided you don't stare for long."

"Sounds lovely." I squinted, leaning against the tree stump. "If they can hide themselves this well, why didn't the one at the library try and conceal its identity?"

"The one at the library was a message." Temper rose and

brushed the dirt from his rear. "The Widow wants us to know he is aware of us."

"How do you know so much about him?" Will asked doubtfully.

Temper's eyes misted over with thoughts from the past and he scrunched his nose. "Much of what was in the past shall remain there. It shall not rear its ugly head in an already defiled world. The Black Widow is no stranger to me. There's a reason I agreed to journey with you. It wasn't out of the kindness of my heart."

I opened my mouth to ask a question which had been burning inside my mind but was cut off by the sound of a deep horn. Our tranquil camp erupted into chaotic confusion as horns blew and the snarls of animals could be heard. Temper was at the edge of camp in an instance, his eyes shaded by his hand.

"They've found us," he growled. "Find your horse and mount up!"

"They've found us?" Will tilted his head. "Who has found us?"

We hurried to our respective steeds and hastily mounted. I turned around in my saddle as Temper mounted his own horse. Behind us and cresting a small hill, several wolves leapt forward. Behind them, three riders in black rode their own mounts over the crest.

"The fell servants of the Black Widow have found us!" Temper snarled. He urged his horse into a gallop as we followed.

We began a desperate ride for the nearing mountains. Temper led the way, his horse a good stride ahead of our own. "There's an old safe house a few miles from here. If we can arrive there unseen, we may yet survive!"

"Survive?" Will cried out. "What will they do to us if they catch us?"

"They will cut you apart and feed you to their wolves," Temper snapped in annoyance. "Shut up and ride, William

Gree, now is not the time for meaningless chatter."

The cold wind yanked at my clothes. Its cold fingers probed my body, and I hunched down in the saddle, trying to make myself a small target. Anthelion's hooves pounded the ground as he ascended the steep terrain, leapt over massive boulders, and weaved around fallen obstacles. Sweat drenched his side and his flanks heaved. Tim, in front, kept his head down, holding to his steed's mane with a death-like grip. An ear-piercing howl rent the morning air and Athillion whinnied in panic. Riding to my right, Katy's mount shook its head in terror. The three horseman and their wolf pack decreased the distance quickly.

"Temper," I bellowed over the howls, "we need to find somewhere to hide! They're catching up!" We tore down a near vertical slope into a valley at breakneck speed.

I watched Katy fumble with the reins as she begged Ultumno to turn. The horse, consumed with terror, ignored its rider and rode under a low hanging tree branch. Katy screamed as she collided with the thick bough. Unable to control her fall, she tumbled down an embankment and landed in a small pond at the bottom of the valley. Tim yanked his mount to a stop and leapt off. Ignoring the dangers arriving behind, he clambered down into the small pond. He splashed his way to Katy's motionless figure. I forced Athillion to a stop. The wolf pack reached the brim of the valley and snarled. Behind them, the riders came to a cantering stop. Temper rode past and put himself between us and the arriving pack.

Will raced down the embankment. Katy lay motionless in Tim's arms

"We have her!" Will yelled. He and Tim supported her unconscious body above the water. "Katy's knocked out. Phoenix, we need you!"

I leapt from the saddle and skidded down the valley side. Beneath my feet, the wet grass gave way to loose stone, and I fell on my rump. When I neared my friends, Katy had already regained consciousness. She mumbled incoherently. As a trio, we brought her out of the water and placed her atop Athillion. Near the valley's edge, Temper swung his broadsword in threatening gestures. The wolves snarled and made attempts to bite his unprotected legs. Temper roared and cleaved the head off one as the rest retreated a few feet. Several dozen yards further behind, the riders watched.

"Begone foul beasts!" Temper commanded. "Flee back to your masters and return hither not. While I yet draw breath, you shall be barred from harming any of my companions. Begone!"

The wolves howled. Ribbons of drool gushed from their mouth, and their eyes bugged out as they circled Temper. They gnashed their teeth and growled. The black-clad riders behind them turned their mounts and rode off. One figure issued a horn blast and the wolves retreated, scampering up the valley wall and out of sight. We watched as they withdrew. Temper sheathed his blade and dashed over.

"Is Katy alright!" Temper cupped his head in her hands and gave her a quick check.

"I'm okay," Katy gurgled. A wide bruise had begun to form over her left eye.

"No broken bones," Temper confirmed. "You don't appear to have a severe concussion. We're lucky. This could have ended far worse than it did. Mount back up, they will return soon. Phoenix take Katy with you on Athillion, he is best able to carry two."

I climbed aboard Athillion, and Temper lifted Katy up in front of me, her head resting against my collarbone. We followed Temper as he rode. We broke the depths of the valley and entered harsh sunlight. All around seemed ominous and full of enemies. Athillion breathed heavily, and I reached down to brush his course flank with my palm. The journey taxed his strength, and it was all he could do to keep in pace with the other mounts. Katy put her arms around my waist and groaned.

"Are you alright?" I gripped her hands with my free hand.

"I feel woozy," she confessed. "Where's Ultumno?"

In the rush to leave the valley behind, I hadn't even thought of her horse. It was just as well that I had nothing to tell her for she closed her eyes.

It was late morning before we'd left the valley far behind. According to Will's calculations and Temper's eagle eyes, we'd traveled enough to be in sight of the safe house. Barely had Temper mentioned this before howls reached our ears. I snapped my head around and watched as a group of snarling wolves leapt over rocks and fallen trees toward us.

Temper dismounted, grabbing his steed's reins and guiding the horse quickly forward. Tim and Will dismounted in turn.

"Quick, everyone, let your horses go wild. They've been trained to return when I bid them. For now, they'll only slow us down and aid in our discovery. Phoenix, help Katy down."

They moved about, fulfilling their tasks with silent determination. I dismounted nimbly. Adrenaline coursed through my body. I didn't want the wolves to be here when it wore off. Temper, sword in hand, leaned against a massive boulder the size of a small home. He murmured a single word and a hidden door groaned outward. Inside was nothing but inky blackness.

"Get inside, now!" Temper bellowed as he drew his sword. The wolves growled and hurled themselves at him. With skill and agility I'd not anticipated, he flung them off and hewed them down with blinding speed. One skinny wolf clamped its iron jaws down on his wrist and shouting, he removed its head from its body.

"Get in!" He roared, gesturing with his sword. Two additional wolves fell at his feet. In the distance, new horns sounded, and I could faintly hear the sounds of horses' hooves against the ground. Reinforcements had arrived.

I helped Katy toward the safe house. She had flung one arm around my shoulders and hobbled slowly. A wolf barreled around Temper and streaked toward us. Snarling, it moved to bite into Katy. I hurled her into the darkness of the safe house and reached for a weapon to fend the beast off. The wolf crashed into me, snapped its jaws and spat drool over me. I felt a hot pain explode in my shoulder, and I screamed in agony. My world turned upside down and I felt my energy escape. The wolf dug its teeth deeper. From above me, someone bashed a rock into the wolf's head. The creature whimpered and released its grip. I gasped and felt the blood flow down my arm. Tim, dropping the rock, gripped my good shoulder and dragged me inside.

Through the hot tears which flooded my vision, I watched as Temper turned and raced for the entrance. Behind him, several wolves snapped at his heels and followed in delirious rage.

"Temper!" I cried out. "Temper, behind you."

Temper ducked as a wolf flew over his head. A second, at his heels, clamped down on his calf and he collapsed to the ground. Will appeared in my vision. He pulled against the heavy stone door and it thudded shut.

"What are you doing?" Tim demanded. He moved to reopen the door, but Will shoved him back.

"Did you not see what those things were capable of?" Will countered. "They completely overwhelmed us. They would have killed Phoenix if you hadn't saved him. Temper is lost. I counted no less than fifteen wolves when he fell and only one of him."

I struggled feebly to rise. The bite in my shoulder flared in agony, and I collapsed back down. At my side, Katy stirred and lifted her head. What should have been a jet-black interior was still lit through some natural opening in the boulder. I could faintly see her silhouette. I reached out and took her hand.

"We'll get through this," I promised. A feeling of helplessness swelled up in my throat, and I swallowed. "We will get out of this alive."

"What are you talking about?" She muttered groggily. "Last thing I remember we were riding..." She paused.

"Temper is out there," Tim stated. "He is giving his life for us and this quest though he barely knows us—and Will just left him for the wolves?"

"You think it was easy condemning him like that?" Will asked. "I did what had to be done to ensure none of us had throats ripped out."

"Guys," Katy called—they stopped their arguing and faced her. "Temper promised to see us to Pikes Peak. He understood the gravity of the situation far better than any of us. You heard him yourself back at first camp. He knows what the Black Widow is capable of, and he still chose to help." She turned to Will. "You can't allow yourself to dwell on your past choices."

From outside, a sudden shout silenced us. Steel clashed with steel and sharp horns blasted through the stone and wood. Accompanying the horns, shouts and rallying cries and the hollow beat of horses' hooves on the mountain floor. Animals yelped and the soft thud of weapons collided with the flesh of wolves. For a moment all went silent. We turned and faced the door. It opened.

▲▼▲▼▲

In the giant cavern, Raul teetered uneasily. He watched as his master received the news. Raul felt the chills run up and down his spine and wondered if this day was to be his last. His predecessor had lasted a mere month before his failures eventually led to his demise. The Widow took the news with no visible outward reaction. His calm exterior and relaxed questions only made Raul's fears worsen. The shade who'd brought the news slunk away. At one end of the chamber, the resident annoyance skulked in the shadows, the red stripes on his cloak shining against the torchlight. Already his parchment was primed as the ink-filled-point hovered over the aged paper. If the Widow ever gave him more power—not that he wanted it—Raul could already imagine a human-free corner of the chamber where the scratching of feather against paper no longer sounded.

"Raul?" The Widow's voice was soft yet controlling, and Raul couldn't stop himself as he stumbled forward. "Raul come to me."

Raul hurried forward, wincing as his master's eyes locked with his own. He saluted with a fist to his chest and bowed in the traditional manner. Raul licked his lips before staring back.

"My lord?" he murmured.

"Give me one reason why I should not order you to the Pit, Raul," the Black Widow said coldly. "I gave you command of my last remaining wolf pack. I do not have the troops to continue this battle if they all bleed headless on the ground."

Raul stammered. "We did not anticipate they would be accompanied this far by the Old One, my lord. Gragchot was rash and overextended himself and in his blindness he—"

"You would put the blame of your failure on a subordinate?" the Widow snarled as he whirled around, his cloak seemed to expand thrice its size and fill the chamber. "You are their commanding officer, are you not?"

"Yes, by your gracious will, of course," Raul stammered. "I simply—"

"Silence!"

The Widow slammed a gloved fist down on his throne. His black cloak returned to its place around his feet. His dead eyes lit with the fiery red against his pale flesh, he seized Raul by the throat.

"You are a failure. If the boy reaches my domain, I will not have the sufficient power to stop him. Get out there, personally, and ensure that he is brought to me in chains. Do what you will with his companions, but bring Temper to me, alive. If you return without them, it will be to your detriment."

Raul was cast off the dais and fell ten feet onto bare stone. Air knocked out, it was a few painful moments before he had enough to respond.

"My liege, it will be as you say. I will go with my best

nightshades and hunt them down. If I return without the boy, I will accept whatever punishment you see fit."

Raul coughed and staggered to his feet. Spots danced before his vision, and a dizzying blur rocked his equilibrium. Blood trickled from a small cut above his eye. He wiped the blood, glanced at it, and grimaced.

"It shall be as you command, my lord!"

To one side the scratch of parchment stopped, and out of the shadows the human stepped. His own cloak swished against the stone. He bowed and strode from the room.

▲▼▲▼▲

We waited in breathless silence.

A sliver of light pierced through the doorway as the door was laboriously swung open. Temper stood in the doorway. His sword was coated with blood, fur, and black mist. The latter clung to his clothes. Behind him, the forest hung in a surreal light. Animal limbs and body parts littered the ground while a horse and its rider lay crumpled against a tree. Black mist hung in the air.

Temper stepped inside the room and shoved the door behind him. He leaned against the inner wall and breathed heavily. For a few seconds no one said anything. We could not help but note his lack of injuries save for the bite on his calf.

"How, I mean..." Will stammered, clearly nervous. "The wolves had you in their jaws. I would never have sealed the chamber if I thought there was a chance of rescuing you."

"You did what you had to," Temper said. "You fear my wrath or perhaps wonder why I appear unscathed; I can see *that* in your gawking faces. None of that is important. I survived, and I had the help of some companions of mine. You all just survived your first encounter with the Black Widow's minions and lived to speak of it."

"Who were the riders?" I coughed. Tim had since covered

my wound in fresh cloth, but the slightest movement made the pain shoot through my spine.

Temper turned to look at me. "You're injured," he stooped and checked my bandages.

"Tim saved my life," I lifted my chin. "A wolf had me in its jaws before Tim bashed it over the head with a stone. I wouldn't be here if it weren't for his bravery."

Temper thanked Tim silently, with a hand to the shoulder, and glanced back. "I thought I had all the wolves focused on me."

"You're good with a blade," Will said. "I've never seen someone move with a sword like that, I mean, not even in *movies*. Where did you learn to do that?"

"As I said," Temper grunted, "my past stays in the past. I lived a separate life when I was young. None of it matters. We need to see some medicine on young Phoenix's wounds before they begin to infect. Tim, do you have the pack from Whipper?"

"No," Tim shook his head, "the pack is still with the horse. I never had the time to remove it during the ordeal."

"No matter," Temper sighed. He reached inside his cloak and withdrew a small pouch. "I still have some of what I brought with me years ago. It'll do enough to close the wound up. Provided you don't agitate it much over the next several days, it'll heal." He opened the pouch and withdrew a small jar.

I watched Katy as they applied the lotion. The blades of pain that shot through me dulled with each stroke of the substance, and I found it less difficult to think. Katy held my gaze, her brown eyes searching through my own.

"Wouldn't it be wise to move camp before reinforcements come to discover what you did to their wolves?" Tim asked. "The blood and corpses will make it obvious where—."

"This is not real stone, although it adopted the properties long ago," Temper said. He ran his fingers over the wall. "A singular material forged centuries past to bewitch the eyes of those around it. Try as they might, those outside who do not realize this is here or what it is will look but not see it for what it is and thus not give it a second thought. The armies of the Widow may march right above our heads and pass a foot away and leave with no more knowledge of our presence than when they first saw it. They may indeed see the bodies of their comrades, but they will assume we forged ahead. The *last* thing they will expect is for us to have lingered here."

We huddled at the back of the room, listening as the wind strengthened. Temper crouched next to me, eyes clenched shut. His sword hung at his feet. To an outsider he looked defeated and lost. Sweat trickled down his muddied face and several torn flaps of fabric now revealed his broken skin. Grime coated his clothing and twigs and leaves had become ensnared in his pockets and lining.

And thus several hours passed

▲▼▲▼▲

"Temper..." I said. "Temper, are you awake?"

"I am now," Temper muttered. He groaned and shifted so as to sit on the unyielding ground. "Is your wound bothering you?"

"No," I said, shaking my head. "How did you survive the attack? Why do you have a sword when a gun would have finished them all a mile off? What is the black mist that hung to your shirt? What were the horns we heard? You talk of allies who saved you, but unless they were the trees themselves, I can't imagine who they were."

"You have a great many question," he said. "Much has been thrust upon you at such a tender age. Where I come from, you are but a bairn. So many questions and filled with a natural curiosity of the unknown. I remember when I was your age. As to the answers, I'm afraid it is not my right to explain everything this world has to offer."

Bairn. Where had I heard that word before?

"Why not?" I asked. "Why are you so against explaining to us what happened in the past?"

Temper's eyes misted over as he stared off. "I left my country, my life, and those I love. It is no easy thing to return to such memories as these. Much of my memory is failing as well. I suppose this comes with old age."

"You're forgetting things?" I cracked a small smile.

"Just a bit," he returned with a chuckle. We both became somber once more. "Phoenix, those wolves and the riders you saw, they are a fraction of what the Widow can send against us."

"Can you tell me at least what nightshades are? You mention them in passing, but I have no idea what you mean."

Tim and Will had since drifted off to mumbling slumber, Katy between them in sleep. Her wound had dried over, and color had returned to her face. I brought my knees to my chest and nodded.

"Nightshades travel through shadows from location to location," he said.

Outside, the wind rose to a rumbling thunder, bashing the trees against each other. Tree limbs crashed to the mountain floor in thunderous booms.

"To understand Nightshades, or Shades as they are often called, you need to understand the property of shadow travel. Shades can bend the shadow and melt themselves into the same properties from which the shadow is made. Where shadows are connected to each other they can move like water along a tilted table. As long as they can travel this way, there is no chance to predict where they will reappear. How far they are able to travel depends entirely on the type of day or at what time they wish to do so. It is an old power, one the Widow bestowed upon them when he made them." His voice began to slur, and his arms hung limp at his sides.

"You look tired," I said. "Rest. We can never truly thank you for saving our lives today both at the library and here. We are in your debt. I'll take the watch."

Before I'd finished speaking, Temper's eyes had once again shut, and his head leaned against the wall. He let go of his sword, which clanged to the floor. I watched his breathing slow until he'd lapsed into sleep. I was left alone with the wailing wind and the darkness, which filled the small room. I situated myself against the door. The steady breathing of my comrades slowed my heart rate, and I began to feel drowsy. The previously unyielding wall now felt more comfortable than a fluffy pillow. It didn't take long before I shut my eyes—a vain promise to myself to reopen them in a few seconds.

▲▾▲▾▲

A blinding light invaded my restful sleep and I blinked rapidly. The injury to my shoulder flared, and I stopped moving. Gingerly, I felt where the wolf's jaws had clamped down. The teeth had dug into my flesh. I was lucky the creature hadn't tried to rip my entire shoulder out.

"My apologies," Temper greeted our sleepy looks. "We must continue our journey."

"No offense, Temper," Tim groaned, "but your safe house could do with some furnishings. I do believe all four of my limbs have fallen asleep and gone on protest."

"You'll have more to complain about than sleeping limbs soon, I don't doubt," Temper heaved the door open and allowed the sunlight to stream in. Outside the scene of chaos and death remained visible. The bodies of headless wolves lay bloating in the sun. I covered my nose.

"Where are we going now?" Katy asked. She'd appeared to have recovered well from her head injury. "And how are we getting there without horses."

"They didn't wander far," said Temper. "They are trained to return at my signal. Fear not, I do believe breakfast will come as the sun dips below in the east." Temper stepped out of the room and we followed, shielding our eyes from the sudden light. He whistled an ear-piercing call and far off the sounds of traveling steeds greeted our ears.

"What time is it?" I asked. The sun was fast approaching the mountains to the west.

"I'd wager we have an hour or so before sunset which makes it roughly five o'clock," Will glanced at the sun.

After a few lengthy moments, the six horses trotted into view. The pack horse, Whipper, led the others and nuzzled Katy's outstretched hand. She patted his nose and rubbed his face. We greeted our mounts.

"Do not trust any animal or being you see," Temper warned, as he vaulted onto his mount. "Any living thing we see could very well be a spy or servant of the Widow. After his first wave was vanquished, he will be more cautious. He doesn't want to completely expose himself to us just yet."

We cantered up the hill behind the safe house and crested onto a plateau. The level plain aided us as we sped into a fierce gallop. A sharp wind had picked up, a freezing annoyance, and I wrapped the blanket that had been given me. The sun's last rays dipped below the mountains and plunged the area into a grey light. Athillion's powerful strides and his bulging muscles slowly rocked me into a state of drowsiness. It didn't take long before I slumped forward, against Athillion's neck, and allowed myself to slip into sleep.

▲▼▲▼▲

A golden glow around me and the slowing of Athillion's movements jolted me awake. My steed slowed from a gallop to a canter to a light trot as Temper raised a fist to slow us down. The entirety of our surroundings had changed from mountainous hills to flat lands as far as I could see. We rode in a line with the rolling hills and mountains to our right and the signs of civilization to our left.

"Why are we so close to the city?" I mumbled.

"Good morning to you," Katy smiled as she gripped her horse's reins. Will rode to the front of the line and spoke with Temper.

"I fell asleep," I rubbed my eyes and pinched myself.

"We've been riding for hours," Katy informed me as she brushed her tangled hair out of her face. "Temper says we have another mile or so left before we need to abandon the horses and proceed on foot. We can't exactly arrive at the Widow's front doors on horseback for all to see."

"Does it concern you at all," I said, "how Temper knows everything about the Widow and where we can find him? If it's this easy to trace our enemy down, why hasn't Temper done so long ago?"

"I trust him." Katy patted her mount's neck and stared at Temper's back as he rode ahead of us. "He is a strange old codger, but I don't believe he is a threat. You saw the way he defended us at the safe house. He risked his life to protect us."

The sun, once descending below the peaks, now rose to our left. The fear of the night fled with the breaking of dawn as another layer of snow covered the ground and our jackets.

"I'm scared." I said, gripping Athillion's reins. "In fact, I'm bloody terrified."

"You'd be a fool not to be," Katy gave me an encouraging smile. "After the wolf attack, I don't know if I'll ever be able to enjoy these views."

We stared appreciatively as the morning sun bathed the soaring peaks and plunging valleys. As far as the eye could see to the east, small groupings of civilization reminded me that we were not far from home. I wondered if my parents were being kept somewhere where they could see these same views—might we all be looking at the same grand vista.

"Temper's not lying," Katy said. "I think I trust him completely. He could have died, and for what? While your quest for your parents is indeed honorable and worth fight for, it's not his fight. He came out of respect for you, Phoenix. We cannot allow ourselves to distrust those who are our allies."

She bowed her head, allowing the folds of her jacket to fall over her face. The chill morning air passed through my own jacket, and I rubbed my exposed hands. Will, deep in thought, meandered from the line and began to descend toward a small city below.

"I think I found a place for breakfast!" He shouted up. We came to a stop as he dismounted and pushed through a wide circle of trees. Planted close together, they offered sufficient cover provided our enemy didn't attack from above.

"I think you're getting a hand for this," Temper said as we followed. "We'll set up camp and rest as long as we are able."

After we'd tied the horses up, Will started a fire. The fingers of the flames shot skyward and melted the snow. The sudden wave of warmth was a relief. In unison, we all sniffed. Katy, on her knees, had placed several long sausages over the crackling logs. The odor of breakfast and the warmth of the fire lowered my concerns. I removed my jacket, placing it over a stump, and sat down. We silently praised Temper's companions for their foresight.

"I never thought a single sausage could taste this good," Katy moaned as she licked her fingers.

"Who knew sitting around a campfire eating sausages could amount to a good time?" Will agreed, staring hungrily at my unfinished breakfast. "You still hungry, Phoenix?"

I felt the rumble in my stomach and shook my head. He gratefully accepted the outstretched sausage and ate. I moved to the edge of the clearing and stared past the trees. Sprawling miles below, a small town stretched out. From one end to the other it couldn't be more than an hour's brisk jog. Smoke curled from chimneys. The cold day continued, and I was stuck in the past. My heart ached. I'd begun to notice the repetitive mood swings whenever I thought for more than a few minutes about my parents. A dull throbbing pounded my chest, and I let a small tear fall. I yearned for a normal life. I desired a life without nightshades and evil masterminds who abducted people's loved ones. I wished for an existence where the most exciting thing to happen revolved around hanging out with one's friends.

"You okay?" Temper laid a rough hand on my shoulder. He stared intently at me.

"Just a bit down," I responded.

"I promised to take you as far as Pikes Peak," Temper said. "I will uphold my promise though I know what we fight against. Nightshades are nothing to laugh about. They are vicious, and when given the chance, they will kill without mercy. They are bred for a single purpose, they fly one banner, and their loyalty is given to one: death. Death flies as their crest. If you take one thing away from all that I have told you, let it be this: show them no mercy, for you shall receive none from them."

I turned and smiled. Though heavy-hearted, I appreciated Temper concern and advice. Glancing at my chattering comrades, I allowed myself an even smaller laugh as I realized that everyone most important to me was with me. I hadn't needed to ask it of them. They'd chosen to journey with me despite the risks. It was my turn to do the same.

"What will we do when we get there?" I asked. "When we arrive at the Widow's front steps, do we knock?"

Temper smiled. "You rescue your parents and you return home."

"Temper, come quick!" Tim's voice was strained.

Our aged guide leapt the clearing in three bounds. At Tim's side, he peered between the branches. Beyond the confines of our enclosed clearing, I heard the sounds of marching. Metal clanged against metal and voices snapped at each other.

"Careful now," Temper admonished as I leaned forward.

Beyond the outstretched fingers of the trees, figures clad all in black marched in unison, their foul odors wafting over the morning breeze. My eyes widened as I gazed at the scene before us. They trudged on. A company of Nightshades thudded by, black-tipped arrows held in quivers on their backs. They carried longbows made with smooth dark wenge. Behind them a regiment of Nightshades cantered along, borne on the backs of mangy horses. A solitary banner snapped in the breeze, carried atop a single spear. I held my breath as the black fabric shifted and revealed the insignia etched onto it. The symbol became clear. It was a red hourglass on a white field with eight black dots circling the field. The mounted Nightshades continued past, revealing a single person behind them. I stared intently.

"He's not Nightshade," Will hissed. The figure, riding a chestnut mare, wore a cloak around his shoulders. A single dagger hung at his waist.

"Who is he?" I muttered softly. "He clearly is human." The figure rode past, head bowed and gloved hands resting lifelessly on the saddle horn. The reins dangled limply from his fingers.

As the company moved past and further down the mountain side, we backed from the tree line. Katy, who had remained behind to extinguish the campfire, stared at us. Her eyes glistened with concern. The smoldering remains of the fire caught my eyes, and I gazed into their smoldering embers. Golden ashes burned. A log popped and caved in two. The smoke dissipated and I watched the final strands blow away. I hugged my arms close and allowed the others to speak.

"The Nightshades are on the move," Temper said. "I have never seen them journey in numbers such as we witnessed. A path has been set in motion, and the best we can hope is for them to lead us to their web. We must follow them."

"Follow them?" Tim wrinkled his nose. "Shouldn't we be attempting to remain as far from them as possible? I don't want to alarm anyone, but if it comes down to a fight, I don't believe I will be of any use."

"I've never held a weapon," Katy nodded, nervously.

"We won't be fighting." Temper vaulted onto his mount and took the reins in his hands.

We followed suit. I gripped Athillion's reins.

Temper grimaced. "We remain in the shadows and we follow them to their master's hidden kingdom. Keep your heads down, be silent and ever watchful, and tread carefully henceforth."

I allowed the others to ride ahead as we broke the cover of the clearing and paralleled the trail the nightshades had been traversing. I marveled at their lack of subtly. Bushes and tree limbs had been hacked apart, and footprints were clearly marked in the soft mud.

"They don't seem to mind if someone discovers them," Will said, as of giving voice to my own thoughts.

"They certainly won't care much longer," Temper agreed. "War is coming."

4 ▸ Strung Up

The night was void and soundless. The usual critter sounds and soft breeze in the treetops had ceased. It worried him. On a night when snow was due to fall with near blizzard conditions, the eerie quiet lent wings to his feet. Forms leered at him from the dark shadows, and he pulled his hood over his face. Mile after mile streaked past as the moon rose and his breath billowed around him. Before long, frost began to cling at his clothing, and he began to lose feeling in his fingers and toes. Rocks crunched beneath his boots, and his cloak swished behind him. He increased his pace. All around, the eerie calmness troubled him. A nagging feeling of dread began to seep into his chest like the enervating damp in his clothing. A cloud passed beneath the moon, and for a brief moment all light faded. Left in utter darkness, he slowed, unsure of his next footing. A twig snapped. A sound that under other circumstances would disturb him not at all now sent shivers down his spine.

Don't let it get to your head, Quire needs you. The cloud passed and the moonlight returned. The shadows reappeared and he continued his hurried journey. A second cloud covered the moon's light, and a second twig snapped off the path in shadow. He whirled about and came to an uncertain stop.

A third twig snapped, the cloud moved, and an arrow appeared out of the night. It flew through the air and imbedded into his shoulder. Gasping, he staggered off the path and pushed through branches laden with dead foliage. The burning pain in his shoulder throbbed, and he groaned. Behind him he detected the sounds of footsteps on the path.

They were coming for him!

He yanked the arrow out and bit down as a scream bubbled up in his throat. He gritted his teeth and clamped a hand over the blood-soaked shirt. A second arrow sank into his back. A third pierced his leg. He collapsed. Barely aware of anything but the pain, he strained his eyes and peered into the darkness before him. He froze as eight orbs slowly illuminated in the center of the darkness. Two red horns shimmered on either side of the eyes. The orbs molded onto a curved face and the horns attached to both sides of its head.

He screamed and rolled away from the Nightshade. The arrow in his leg snapped in half as he spun over. The arrowhead dug deeper. Blood coated him and the leaves beneath as he floundered, a fish out of water. The Nightshade appeared fully from the shadows, a glowering beast eight feet tall and red as the blood pouring from his wounds. It knelt and removed a curved dagger from its belt.

"Do it," he said.

His eyes rolled back into his head as the pain grew with the arrival of a fourth arrow in his side.

The Nightshade placed the dagger to the man's throat and slashed. A single cry later, the man lay motionless, a dark liquid now stained his white cloak.

▲▼▲▼▲

We rode with great care as the horde of Nightshades moved. Their scouts ranged far from the main host, so we rode farther. Barely detectable save for a crushed bush or forgotten piece of leather, they moved as a black sea over parched land. Snow had begun to fall as the day waned and grew colder. Prints covered by freshly fallen snow, they became harder to track. Temper often dismounted and studied the terrain before mounting and urging his steed in a new direction.

I pulled my blanket around me and ducked my head under its protective covering. The clear flakes melted upon contact, but more came, and the air grew colder. Athillion and the other horses seemed unfazed by the cold weather front—while their human counterparts began to shiver, yearning for the warmth of home.

"I didn't realize how cold it gets up here," Tim's teeth chattered against each other as he blew into his hands.

"It's like a different world," Will agreed as he sniffed. His nose red, he'd been the least vocal about the uncomfortable temperatures. "Honestly though, I like it. The pure white of the snow and the soaring peaks makes this place almost magical, if you forget the abominations we are following and why we are out here in the first place." His breath fogged in front.

"Do you think we're lost?" Tim murmured as he slowed to allow me to ride at his side. "We haven't had a sign of the horde since earlier, and Temper hasn't dismounted in a bit."

"Maybe that's a good sign," I said. Blurred by the falling snow, Temper was focused on the path ahead. "If he hasn't had to check, maybe we are close."

The once light snowfall had changed as the snowflakes grew in size and quantity. It became nearly impossible to see more than a few feet ahead of us. I felt the weight of gathering snow atop my blanket and shook it.

"Make for the overhang!" Temper's voice sounded far off as he turned to look at us. Gesturing wildly, he pointed to where a stony outcropping had come into view. Beneath the stone. Needing no encouragement, we steered our mounts to intercept.

I tethered Athillion to a thick trunk and staggered beneath the rock overhang. As the others trickled in and shivered in their cold and wet garments, Temper began to make preparations for camp.

"The Widow seeks to prevent us." He grimaced. "This is no natural weather. It is burdened with the weight of evil. I fear we must wait this snowfall out. It is useless to plod ahead further while we catch our death."

"We have nothing to start a fire," Will announced as he went through the packs on Whipper's back. "Everything is damp and cold. If we can't start a fire, we may find ourselves the newest popsicle flavor by morning."

"Your optimism is greatly appreciated," Temper snapped. Rubbing the bridge of his nose, he sighed. "If there is no fire, we must use what we have for warmth. Are any of the blankets dry?"

Will shook his head and the two began to argue over accommodations. Meanwhile, I drifted over to where Katy and Tim had plopped themselves at the back of the outcrop. Open on three sides to nature, the overhang offered little comfort from the cold wind outside and the snow accumulation.

"Mind if I join the company?" I squatted and smiled. The simple act of smiling seemed foreign.

"Your body heat is greatly appreciated," Katy smiled back.

"Just my heat?" I sat down, keenly aware that our shoulders touched. "I was hoping my entire presence would be welcomed."

"If it makes you feel any better," Tim said, leaning forward, "she said I could join her because my hair is like a natural umbrella and offers shelter from the wind."

"I feel used." I forced a hoarse laugh.

"Come on," Katy shook her head. "I didn't mean any of that. I'm just cold. I didn't realize that adventures often come with such unpleasantries as this."

"I wonder what happened to the nightshades," I said.

"They probably love this weather," Tim said. "I bet when the dark cold snow comes, they celebrate. What better time to kill or kidnap than when the sun sets early and the snow drives people in?"

"I'm sure we'll find where Phoenix's parents are," Katy said and gave my hand a reassuring squeeze.

"The more we delve into the mountains, the more I worry

if it was worth it." The confession felt like a weight being lifted from my chest. Even the cold couldn't keep me from treating a sigh of relief.

"What do you mean?" Katy tilted her head.

"With the wolf attack and now being forced to claim shelter in such places as this..." I glanced about. "Well, I can't help but wonder if this was all a mistake. Of course, I want to save my family and restore what once was, but at what cost? If you all die of frostbite, it's not like I'll be able to sleep regardless of who returns home with me."

"I hear that," Tim said. "We all love our parents, but losing any of you would be hard."

"You shouldn't be worried about us," Katy admonished softly. "We have Temper, and he knows what he is doing."

Will came and sat down next to Tim. "Nightshades aren't a thing to causally ignore. We heard what they are capable of with their shadow travel. Last thing I want is to wake up and see a nightshade slitting my throat."

"Not helping the mood, Will." Katy glared at him.

"He's right," I took her hand in mine and we leaned against each other as the wind began to howl outside. "The nightshades and the Black Widow know we exist, and it won't be long before they find us. Temper can't fend them all off, not on his own."

"I wonder if Temper can show us how to fight," Katy mused.

"The art of killing one of those creatures is simple enough," Temper finally spoke. Quiet as he'd been, he turned from watching the snow and rubbing his horse's neck. "You're right to desire to learn how to defend yourselves. As Phoenix said before, these creatures aren't something to shrug off. Shadow travel has ended countless lives."

"Will you teach us?" I asked.

"Aim for their neck or torso," Temper responded. "Their weakest points are those two areas."

"That's great to know," Will returned. "However, we have no weapons."

Temper produced four small blades from his cloak and handed them to us. Silvery blades stuck into wooden handles—they looked more cutlery than a weaponry.

"In a pinch they will save you. It's the most I have for now, but where we are heading, we may not need even these." He moved back to the overhang and stared silently into the whirling snow.

The storm raged on as we slumped in cold defeat. Our clothes became like wet tarps stuck to our skin. The others having lapsed into weary sleep, I fiddled with the knife handed to me. A small carving had been etched into the handle. The more I gazed at it the less it made sense. I was about to close my eyes and join the other's in blissful sleep when I heard a soft hum.

> *Her eyes moonlit lights of old sparkle as memories grow cold*
> *Depths of time and eras unfold ere the darkness curse her soul*
> *Her hair in golden light doth bathe the stars around her as a crown*
> *Golden robes ascend the throne as deceit plunders all around*
> *Her footprint goes throughout all time as armies clash for her name*
> *Death defiles and tribulation triumphs o'er all who claim that fame*
> *Men to battle and women to care for the future hope she sees*
> *A grassland erect and proud engulfed by rotten splintered trees*
> *Her image is one of timeless beauty against the choler of woe*
> *Darkness may shield the light from all but corrupt the depraved foe*
> *Her fame as time began in old side by side through halls of gold*
> *Ere the world extinguish and time snuffs out and stories therein told*
> *Her eyes moonlit lights of old sparkle as memories grow cold*
> *Depths of time and eras unfold ere the darkness curse her soul*

I sat up and stared through the darkness to where Temper leaned against rock. The snow had ceased, and the wind had calmed. Beyond his dark silhouette, the mountainside had been blanketed in a thick layer of white beauty.

"There is hope yet," I heard him sigh. "Hope still exists in the High City."

"What were you singing about?" I leaned on one elbow, conscious of the sharp stone beneath me. "It was a beautiful song."

"It's called the Lay of Ëónë." He watched the moon as it slowly rose in the sky. "It's where I used to live."

"I've never heard of that country."

"It's not exactly a country." Temper hugged his arms around himself. "But it exists outside my ability to return."

"It was beautiful." I stood and crossed to his side. The frigid temperatures caused me to momentarily lose my breath. "You should come closer to the back of the cave. It's absolutely freezing here."

"Is it?" Temper seemed to realize for the first time of the temperature and shivered.

"When this is all completed and we're at home sipping cups of coffee over a blazing fire and watching the snow fall heavily outside," I said, "when that happens, I expect you to tell me everything from your past. You're an enigmatic soul."

"The world doesn't have time for my ramblings." Temper smiled. "But I promise you if we survive this, I'll do my best, provided the coffee has some creamer in it."

We shared a quiet chuckle and moved to the back of the cave. Temper drew his cloak about his body as he eased himself to the ground.

"I still think about home and school and what it was like before we went plunging headfirst into the mountains with no agenda beyond finding my parents." I leaned back against the wall.

"Time cares for no one," Temper said. "It will run right over you and not even look back. Those below the mountain are completely oblivious of the goings on just miles above their safe walls and roofs. The Black Widow waits and watches. He bides his time for the opportune moment to strike."

"You make it sound so hopeless."

"It is," Temper's grim words rattled me. "I've fought against him in the past."

"But you survived," I said. "There must be a way to defeat him if you survived."

"I survived because I was allowed to." Temper closed his eyes, the pain of the memory growing.

I settled into an uneasy rest that gripped us all. Outside, the white world shone in splendor as the moon rose high, majesty of the night. Clouds moved overhead, interspersed with the occasional glimpse of night sky. Trees whispered, lulling us to sleep with their ancient tales.

▲▼▲▼▲

The cavern reeked of brooding fear, and Raul waited in silence at the small door. Ears pricked, he strained his eyes into the inky blackness. No light penetrated the rotting evil that resided here. It had begun to creep into the bones of the mountain and upward to the trees and living things above. It had corrupted and twisted the minds of man and beast alike who walked its hillside and made a home in its passageways. A sickness which had no cure resided over one of the most famous mountain peaks. At its heart, a room of hardened malice waited. Over the years, the Black Widow's patience had slowly lessened. No one left this place alive. He understood it was only a matter of time. Strangely though, he felt satisfied.

"Do you fear your fate so that you sulk in the safety of silence?"

The words were calculated and cold. The voice originated from the center of the black dais, which blended perfectly into the surrounding darkness. A single red light illuminated the obsidian throne. Two red hourglass symbols had been crudely painted on the armrests. Upon its hardened seat, the Widow sat. In the glare of the red light, Raul could make out the black cloak around his master's shoulders. Emblazoned with the hourglass, it was one of the few articles of clothing the Widow never removed.

"My liege." Raul bowed deeply and placed a fist to his chest.

"What news from the east?" the Widow asked. "What of the boy and his companions? What of the old one?"

"We found no evidence of the boy's whereabouts. The nightshade who escaped the first attack rode at my side, to guide us to the site of the massacre. What we encountered there was a perfect scene of the creature's report. Your grimwolves lay butchered over the field. We found the hidden safe house they sought refuge in and some of our wolves detected human blood inside. I marched the remainder of my party south. We faced some resistance from a group of Grey Cloaks and lost a number of my shades."

"In the entirety of your report, I hear nothing but loss." The Widow stood, his eyes their usual blackness. Raul hastily stepped back. The Widow advanced. "Far better would it have been for you to die in the mountains engaged in combat than on the fields of cowardice."

Raul's stomach lurched, and sweat began to trickle down his forehand and into his eyes. He shook in his leather boots.

"If it please you, my lord," he stammered, "our heavy loss did not come without significant reduction of their forces as well. We numbered eighty slaughtered on the South Road. The company of the boy vanished a mere mile from that location. We have a general area to search and I have my best shades investigating diligently. We will not disappoint you!" His entire life had been dedicated in service to the Widow. No one survived who served the Black Widow.

"Seize him!"

The order came suddenly. Caught off guard, Raul was unable to defend himself as two burly nightshade guards seized either arm and roughly forced him to his knees. The Widow slowly advanced. In his hand he held a curved dagger. The serrated edge appeared recently sharpened. Raul heaved and flexed, swinging his legs in any direction he could.

"I was only following your orders," Raul desperately struggled. "I have been nothing if not loyal since you arrived from beyond. It was I who welcomed you with open arms and brought you to this place. Unhand me, you demons!" The last words were directed with rage to the nightshades who held him in a vice-like grip.

"Bring him." The Widow strode past, cloak swishing out behind. The nightshades heaved Raul to his feet and dragged him kicking and shouting out of the cavern.

Upon entering a small chamber, Raul noticed the heavy odor of dried blood. It was not often that he feared death, for he lived with the possibility of dying every day. Today, however, he yearned for freedom, to feel the sun once more on his flesh, to smell the flowers in bloom, to watch the bustle of life that sat at the foot of the mountain. He suddenly realized how much he still wanted to accomplish. In an attempt to bite the hand holding him, he noticed a pit had been dug at the center of the chamber.

"What is that?" He stretched his neck to see better. "What are you doing with me?"

Raul was roughly dragged to its edge and a blade placed at his neck. The notched metal forced several drops of blood out over the empty space. The illusion of no bottom sent goosebumps racing up his arms and back. Several small holes had been carved into the stone. From these, a steady stream of fuzzy black bodies moved up and down. Raul realized why the base of the pit appeared to have no floor.

Raul, eyes wide with absolute terror, surged against his captors. Spittle flew from his mouth. Adrenaline coursed through his body, and spots danced across his vision. He flexed his muscles once more and heaved all of his weight against the iron grip of his captors.

"You cannot do this!" he roared. His muscles tensed as the nightshades pushed him toward the edge. "You cannot commit me to a death such as this! I am loyal to you and to the Hourglass to which I pledged my life. I am loyal! You cannot do this!"

With a single prod, the nightshades let go. Raul felt time slow as he tipped over the edge. He had a moment to see that the bottom of the pit moved in thousands of legs and bodies. Several small hourglasses glared up at him, as if reminding him of who he had failed. Hands flailing, he grasped for any projection that would slow his fall.

His screams and distressed cries echoed throughout the chamber. His body was instantly covered in a sea of black and red, and the Widow watched as the flailing limbs twitched in convulsions. The hundreds of thousands of arachnids, flooding over the fresh food, spun thin strands around the body until it resembled a cocoon.

The Widow gestured wordlessly, and the nightshades climbed into the pit. Without any visible cue of fear, they knelt into the swarm of creatures and retrieved Raul's lifeless body. They tore away the cocoon of death the spiders had spun around him. The body restored, they climbed back up. The spiders that had attached to them fell away and disappeared into the darkness. They presented the corpse. Kneeling, the Black Widow reached out a hand and touched Raul's bloodless cheeks. Puncture wounds covered his body in every conceivable area so that his form was full of small holes. White as a ghost, Raul lay. Where blood once ran in abundance, the empty veins filled black, lines snaking across his body. With a single word, the Widow stood and turned to leave the chamber. Raul's eyes opened.

5 · The Hour at Hand

I yawned. A harsh light forced itself beneath my eyelids, and I groaned in protest. Blinking rapidly, I shielded my eyes from the intense sunlight as it bounced from snow pile to drift. The morning had arrived. I moaned as my body ached from the stone floor. I glanced to where the others still slept and stopped. Katy, at some point in the night, had crossed silently and now lay next to me. She breathed softly in her sleep. Next to her, Temper's head hung on his chest as he sat against the wall. His hand gripped the sword he had used against the wolves.

I rose and tread across the floor to the overhang's opening. The morning was crisp, and the sounds of running water were evident. Snow melted and trees shook off their heavy weights. Showers of glistening snow floated across the mountainside. It was peaceful in a way I'd never imagined.

"I fell asleep." Temper's voice startled me. "I should have stood watch, but my wretched body couldn't keep awake."

"You're not to blame," I said. "We all needed sleep. This travel has been taxing on us all."

The group began to move in varying stages of wakefulness as we prepared to break camp. No signs of nightshades, Temper guided us from the overhang and through the crunchy snow. Tim dipped a hand into the fluffy pile and greedily ate it. Breakfast from the day before seemed like an eternity ago.

The horses remained tethered to the trees we'd tied them to, and with practiced agility, we mounted. Blankets and coats tightened, we began the trek onward. Apprehensive of every shadow, we soon found the path and started making up for lost time. The snowfall of the day before had led to a lengthy delay that bombarded me with concern. Thoughts about what my parents were going through caused my temple to throb. Not even the cold of the mountain snow could aid my swirling thoughts. I pictured my father chained to a rock and whipped. At his side, my mother begged the nightshades to spare his life and take hers. I moved my lips wordlessly as I imagined her cries for mercy as my dad cried out in agony.

"You've been quiet," Katy said. She rode by my side. After an hour of hard riding, we'd begun to make noticeable progress. Even Temper seemed to brighten. Katy waited for me to respond.

Tim had begun to lag further and further behind, his horse sweating profusely. I turned my head to call for him to hurry forward before we lost sight of him, when Glas stumbled. Tim tumbled off and slammed into a boulder. He lay unmoving. I spun Athillion around and prepared to ride to his side and render aid. Before I could, Temper rode beside me and seized Athillion's reins.

Without pausing, I hastily dismounted, feeling the horse's coarse hair scratch against my thighs. I landed hard, the frozen ground slamming into my soles. Breath taken, I raced down the crumbling hillside as trees whipped at my face. I stumbled as I landed on gravel, which gave way in crumbling disarray. Behind me Katy called out a warning. Turning around, I noticed Temper's body a second before he collided with me. We tumbled and rolled down the hillside. I cursed and reached for anything to break my fall. All around me, rubble and pebbles rained down. Above, the horses stampeded, breaking what meager control anyone had over them and hurtling down the mountain and toward flat land. Below, Tim began to stir in the initial wakeful moments of confusion and massaged his head. Having come to a complete stop, I groaned and rose shakily. My arms and legs a canvas of broken skin and deep blue bruises, I turned to run the final distance. Temper, once more, launched himself into me and we came to a crashing stop inside of a prickly bush. I cried in pain as thorns stuck to my skin and hair.

"Temper what in blazes do you—"

He clamped his hand over my mouth and glanced up. I realized that all had gone silent. A few moments later, after the dust had wafted off to join the clouds in the sky, a black silhouette moved above. Caught in the rays of the sun, its shadow covered us. The head moved as if looking to each side before seemingly floating over our hideout and vanishing. I turned my head to peer through the branches of the bush and thanked Temper silently for this place to crash into me. A few feet to either side would have left us vulnerable. Hidden, I took comfort knowing that a surprise attack was a possibility should our situation turn sour.

Through the thin branches, I peered out as the figure went from shadow to a physical form. Dagger drawn, the creature approached where Tim had fallen. I couldn't help but note the dried blood on its serrated edge. Gaining my unspoken promise, Temper removed his hand from my mouth and shifted slightly to see down the slope better. I place my lips as close to his ear as possible.

"We have to distract them," I whispered. "Tim doesn't know how to defend himself."

As I said this, Tim rose into view, his dreadlocks flying about as he swung a sturdy branch. Several other Nightshades had joined the first and they surrounded him. Tim swung with fury and fear. A Nightshade took a jab at his back as he swung away. Crying out, Tim fell to one knee. A second Nightshade jabbed his sword into Tim's unprotected shoulder. A third advanced and backhanded Tim onto his back. It took every ounce of my being to refrain from bursting from cover and, screaming, descend into the skirmish. Temper, hand on his sword hilt, shook his head. For now, Tim would have to fight alone. My stomach plummeted as I imagined his pain at being seemingly abandoned for dead.

The Nightshades yanked Tim to his feet, and one slammed the pummel of his curved sword between Tim's eyes. My friend dropped, head falling back. I winced as I imagined the crunch of bone, but Tim let no sound out. He lay on his back, staring up at the heavens. I choked as my stomach seemed to lurch into my throat. Further uphill, I imagined Katy, protected by Will, hiding, feeling intense flashes of desire to save Tim. The band of Nightshades examined the fallen boy before grabbing him and slinging him over a shoulder like a sack of rocks. The nightshade carrying him let out a grunt and sheathed its blade.

Temper, eyes glued to the band, moved stealthily forward. He kept low as he exited the bush and began to slink along the ground, moving from trees to boulder to bush. I watched as he slowly crept closer. Numbering eight, the nightshades moved and began to hurry back the way we'd come. I ducked my head into the depths of the shadows as they passed rapidly. Their movements sent a hailstorm of gravel and pebbles raining down on my head as I bit my tongue. We waited for what felt like an eternity before Temper rose from behind an oak tree and hurried toward me. Sensing our safety, I rose from the bush, no longer concerned for my own pain, and rushed toward where Will and Katy had last been. They were no longer in sight.

"Where are Will and Katy?" I hissed at Temper as he sped past.

Our guide reached the latest portion of the hillside moments before I did. I laboriously made the final feet and stared at what Temper was gazing at. Curled into a ball, Will held Katy as they lay behind a wide boulder.

"The danger has past," Temper announced. "They have your friend."

Katy rose, brushed off her shirt, and wiped a tear way. "Why didn't you stop them?"

"I am sorry, but their numbers and knowledge of the area far surpasses my own." Temper raised his hands apologetically.

"As the only member with an actual sharp weapon, I would have quickly fallen to their swords. Had I tried to rescue Tim, we all would have perished or worse been taken to the Black Widow himself."

"Maybe that would have been for the better," I murmured as a thought began to bubble inside.

"You do not want to be his prisoner." Temper's words were harsh yet full of concern. "The Widow is not known for his kindness and certainly not toward people he deems a threat or a potential breach in his plans. Had we gone before the Widow we would have no hope of rescuing your parents and now Tim. Our only hope for survival is to sneak into his domain and return with what we came for, nothing more. We all agreed upon the risks when setting out on this journey. Tim knew it, for I spent hours urging him to remain behind and outlining the risks he'd be enduring."

"We can't do nothing," Katy said. "There has to be a way we can save him. You managed to survive wolves and Nightshades on horseback. How come you couldn't do the same here?"

"What if being taken in is the best way to get close to my parents?" I muttered.

"I had aid in that defense," Temper responded to Katy. "Besides, wolves are a creature I'd much rather pit myself against than Nightshades. The foul creatures of the Pit are inhumanely strong with tactics that outsmart some of the greatest swordsmen. Trust me when I tell you that remaining hidden and letting Tim be captured, even momentarily, was the only way any of us were leaving that scene alive and unharmed."

"Quiet!" I cried out. I felt the onset of a headache and rubbed my throbbing temple. Sun reflected bright off the melting snow—the bright light jabbed at my eyes. Cloudless, the sky shone a brilliant blue.

"What is it?" Katy asked.

"If we get ourselves captured and transported to the Black Widow's hideout, wouldn't that put us one step closer to those we're trying to rescue? Temper, you know our foe. Tell me, would they bring us to their dungeon first?"

"Phoenix," Temper's voice dropped, "your heart is in the right place, but I'd rather you remain alive than risk your heart being presented to the Widow as a sign of your death. The Nightshades will, unless ordered otherwise, kill any who trespass close to the borders of their master. We are in their land, and every step from henceforth must be calculated and careful. We cannot simply allow ourselves to be taken prisoner and expect to survive long enough to save even ourselves. If you want to save your parents and Tim, we must do so secretly."

"You're saying there is no other option than sneaking up to the front door?" I winced as my headache flared.
"Our only safe chance lies with such a strategy," Temper said. He looked with concern as I rubbed my forehead repeatedly.

"It's decided then," Will said. For the first time since Tim had been taken, he gazed up from his perch at the top of the slope. Eyes red with unspoken grief, he gave a determined, grim smile. "These Shades have now taken someone from all of us. We move further west until we find and successfully rescue those who we came for."

A solitary horn resonated over the mountain peaks. We stared about. From beyond the peak above us, came a second horn, closer than the first. Temper, alarmed, grabbed my shoulder and we raced toward the sound. The sounds of footsteps marching in unison caught my ear, and I sprinted faster, hoping Temper's allies had come to help. We crested the mountain side and gazed down its opposing incline.

Below, marching as a black tide of death, nightshades moved in rhythm, marching so their footsteps thudded like a heartbeat. The horn sounded a third time and a red nightshade on a steed moved into view. He turned and looked in our direction. I ducked below the ridge line, holding my breath. Will, Katy, and Temper also flattened themselves to the moist grass.₉₀

"What do you think is happening?" Will hissed as he raised his head just enough to peek one eye over. "They have Tim!" His exclamation sent shivers down my spine, and I lay my cheek to the ground. Sounds became muffled as I closed my eyes.

"This is good," Temper's response forced my eyes open. I stared in disbelief.

"Good?" I demanded. "What is good about my friend being in their hands? He only came because Will couldn't keep his mouth shut about our travel plans." The stress coupled with the pulsating migraine sent my thoughts whirling around in my head.

"My mouth shut?" Will's was hurt and angry. "Tim knew something was up, and when he asked, I couldn't just lie to him."

"Sometimes you have to lie," I said. "Sometimes a lie is the best course of action when life or death is on the line."

"Will didn't intend for Tim to get taken." Katy placed a hand on the small of my back in an attempt to reassure me. "For that matter, none of us planned for any of this to happen. You can't blame Will for what Tim chose to do. Tim chose to come."

"Yeah, I know." I gave an apologetic nod. Will returned the gesture.

"Do you feel well?" Temper crawled over, ensuring his entire body remained below sight of the marching horde below. "You've been acting odd since Tim's capture."

"Maybe this whole trip is just emotionally affecting me." I said through gritted teeth. The pain in my head grew, so I pounded my fists against my skull. "My head is about to split apart." My vision went red. I felt my eyes roll back into my head.

"Get him on his back." The order was muffled, and I murmured softly to myself as the pain intensified beyond any pain I'd ever felt. Down below, the sounds of several horses thundering up the ridge perked my ears. I struggled to move, but Temper held me down on my back.

"We're exposed out here," Katy said. "We need to find cover."

"This can't be possible," Temper muttered as he grabbed snow and placed it on my forehead. The cooler temperature instantly began to clear the fog in my head.

"Katy's right," said Will, "we need to move."

Temper scooped me in his arms and hurried us to a clump of bushes. Before we reached it, the sun drew a shadow of a humanoid form in front of us.

"Quickly!" Temper hissed. Will pushed forward and dove into the bush, followed quickly by Katy. Last to enter safety, Temper placed me down and pulled the branches back together.

I gurgled out a scream as the pain returned. Hot flashes rode through my body, and I wiped sweat from my face. Temper applied snow to my head. We all quieted as two mounted forms appeared in our vision.

"I heard something," a nasally voice stated. "Someone was up here."

"Why didn't you shadow travel?" A scratchy voice demanded. "If someone was up here, they heard our arrival and fled. Next time, use what brain you still have left."

"It's not my fault the Hourglass haven't been able to cast their spell on these dreadful beasts."

"Shut it," the second voice hissed. "You speak bad about the Hourglass, and next you'll end up like the Assistant."

The two nightshades returned in the direction they'd come. I breathed deeply, practicing my exercises.

"What's wrong with Phoenix?" Katy asked when she was sure no enemies were around to hear.

"I've only seen this happen once," Temper was tight lipped as he examined me. "When those of a specific importance were in close proximity to a member of the Hourglass. Their polar opposites of good and evil collided and created an internal battle the likes of which we can only imagine. Quick, supply me with more snow. We need to get his temperature down quickly."

"What happened to the previous individual?" Will sounded nervous.

"He survived and lives an old hermit," Temper said, and began to feel the pain diminish. "Phoenix, can you hear me?"

"The pain has gone," I opened my eyes and appreciated the lack of agony at the bright sun. "I don't know what came over me."

Will and Katy took turns explaining everything I'd missed. Temper restated his previous assessment of my pain.

"Special bloodline?" I stood from our cover and peered around. "I'm not part of a special bloodline."

"We'll discuss this later." Temper hurried to the ridge line. Below, the flood of nightshades had diminished to a single stream as they marched single file in a small gulch. Led between two burly brutes, Tim stumbled. Shackles had been clamped around his wrists, and a long chain led to a nightshade bringing up the rear.

Then it came to me.

"I know how we will find the Widow." my eyes widened. "Tim will lead us."

We watched in silence as the last of the Shades turned beyond our sight. The mountainside returned to its natural beauty and the birds began to sing. It was as if a blanket of darkness had been lifted and life had been allowed to return to the mountains.

"It just might work," Will rubbed his chin. "It's too dangerous for all of us to be captured but Tim, unknowingly, might just be the key we need."

"What happens to Tim is now outside of our control unless we can arrive unharmed and safely," Temper said. "It will be no small feat sneaking beneath their defenses for they will be on high alert, now that one of Phoenix's company is in their possession."

"You make him sound like a slave," Katy wrinkled her nose.

"My dear girl," Temper grimaced, "being a slave would be the best we could hope for. They will not treat him kindly."

I led the charge as we slid and skidded down the

mountainside in the direction the host had disappeared. Safety our priority, we kept to the clumps of trees and tall bushes to conceal us should nightshades morph from the shadows or ride into the clearing. Sun beginning its slow descent above us, we reached the gulch and began scurrying along it, careful to keep off the dried clay bed. Trees poked their reaching fingers into our jackets and hair, and rocks aimed to trip us.

It the gathering dusk we saw fires lit under watchful eyes. Having made camp, the nightshades posted guards on every conceivable approach.

"Dammit," I said. "There's no possible way we can save Tim before he is taken inside the belly of the beast, we'd need to be virtually invisible to even consider it."

"We make camp here," Temper said. "Will and I shall take first watch. Katy, you and Phoenix will take the second. Keep your weariness at bay for you must be alert. We are in the Widow's domain now, and all order and law we may have once expected are to be ignored. Stay alert!"

I scrunched up my jacket and leaned my head against it as Temper and Will took their positions at the edge of our small camp. Cold and cramped, I wrestled with the day's events. Tim's capture meant the Black Widow would be firmly aware of our impending arrival. It also meant he could use my friend as a means to force our hand. I tossed and turned, sleep feeling like a luxury I couldn't indulge in. By my side, equally distressed, Katy stared up between the tallest tree canopies, her eyes fixated upon the glinting stars as night took hold.

"Do you think Tim is okay?" she murmured for the eighth time as I shifted position. I glanced at her.

"I don't pretend to have much hope," I said. "Tim is strong. He'll do what he must to survive and I can't fault him for it."

"You think he'll give our information to the Widow?" Katy broke her stare with the heavens and turned to look at me. We gazed into each other's eyes as the distant sounds of bellowing and shouting lofted over the soft breeze. For a moment I felt the urge to say something but held back.

"From what Temper says, it sounds like the Black Widow has means and tools to ensure his prisoners give him the information he needs. It's not a matter of if but when. Tim is strong, like I said, but no one can be strong forever against pure evil. It's up to us to save him. I'm the one that got him into this."

"You sure make me feel *so* much better." Katy chuckled, her hair falling over her face.

"I do what I can with the talents I'm given," I returned her smile. "Sometimes that's all one can do, y'know? We're stuck in a world of chaos and evil and death and we're expected to paint on a happy face and not break character. The closer we get to the Widow's hideout, the more I begin to feel the crippling fear take place."

"I'm terrified," Katy's eyes glistened as tears welled up. I moved closer, putting one arm around her shoulder. She rested her head on my chest and together we stared up at the peaceful night sky. The final rays of light had faded beyond the mountains. Only the light from the far-off camps signaled the presence of humanity.

"Honestly," I began, "I'd be concerned if you weren't. When we started this trip—it feels like forever ago—I knew we might never return. But a piece of me always held onto the hope that just maybe we'd be lucky, like the characters in some of your books. The characters who are given plot armor and can walk into a trap laid by fifty men and return with barely a scratch to be had. Part of me wished that it would be akin to a simple stroll down the lane where we'd pick up my parents and return."

"It's never like that." Katy yawned, snuggling closer. "Is it?" She closed her eyes.

"Oh, to live in a world of fiction." I too yawned. "What it would be like to live in a world where the choices between right and wrong were labeled with highlighters and consequences were a thing of the past."

I glanced down as I realized she'd begun to softly snore. I

wished I could protect her from all dangers and bring her home. If I'd been given the chance to return home and bring Katy safely back to her mother at that point, I couldn't guarantee I wouldn't have taken it.

Beyond us, Temper leaned against a thick spruce while Will began whittling with his pocketknife. The flickering lights in the distance became a mesmerizing illusion as I fantasized that the shadows formed into nightshades and the glint of the moonlight against their swords and spears showed a glimpse of what was to come.

▲▼▲▼▲

I awoke with a jolt as Will nudged my arm. Rubbing my eyes, I rose softly, waking Katy, and tiptoed to the edge of camp. The night had grown cold, so I placed my jacket around my shoulders. Temper remained in the same spot I'd seen him at before drifting off.

"All quiet?" I rubbed my arms and glanced in the direction of the nightshade camp.

"Not a stir of movement," Temper wearily stood and trudged to a small log. "Their fires died out an hour ago. I don't believe they are aware of our presence." His voice trailed off as he slumped against the wood and shut his eyes. Will, equally tired, had already fallen asleep.

Katy stood by my side, sleepy. For several long moments neither of us spoke as we gazed out at where we imagined the nightshade guards stood silently. I wondered what they thought about as they stood motionless for hours on end.

"I hope Tim is okay," Katy said, breaking the silence. "Will told me that it appeared all quiet over there."

"Temper said the same." I squeezed my eyes shut. When I opened them, I stepped back in alarm. A single orange light burned in the darkness. I hissed. "Get down!"

We crouched and watched as a form shrouded in a cloak

stood at the edge of the camp. As quickly as the light's arrival, I began to feel the headache return. A sensation of pure agony began to pound in my temple, and I dropped to all fours, moaning. The figure moved from the camp and out of its protection. It headed in our direction.

"Are you okay?" Katy frantically poked at my face. I batted her hand away as the pain blinded me.

"Get down!" I urged as the last of my strength left me. Katy lay prone on the ground. I felt blindly in the dark until I gripped a thick twig. Placing it between my teeth, I bit down hard.

The cloaked form passed by and vanished into the inky blackness. As it moved further away, I began to feel the pain diminish until it was a manageable soreness.

"What happened?" Katy stared at me, her eyes wide with concern and fear.

"I don't know," I said. My voice sounded strange. "My head just exploded with pain again."

▲▼▲▼▲

I allowed our companions several precious hours of sleep before I shook them awake. They rose without complaint or nourishment for time was not on our side. We'd agreed to move early in hopes of gaining an advantage.

"Let's hope my theory works," Temper kept low to the ground.

We moved silently and swiftly from tree to tree as we passed the nightshade encampment. It wasn't long before we stopped to rest. I divulged the information from our night shift to Temper. He remained mute as I described the cloaked figure and my skull splitting headache.

He cursed softly. "This does not bode well. I think I know what is happening, the relation of your headaches to certain members of the Widow's force."

"What is happening?" I asked.

"There is an ancient bloodline which can trace its roots back to the beginning of time itself," Temper began. "They are the oldest clan with a long history of royalty."

"Royalty?" I touched my neck subconsciously. "What are you talking about? I asked about my headache and that cloaked figure, not to be given a history lesson on kings and bloodlines."

"See, *this* is your problem," Will bit off the end of his last bar and shook the food at me. "You ask a question, and when a response is given, you ignore it because it doesn't fit with what you were anticipating."

I at least had the decency to act annoyed. In reality, my thoughts were a basket of turmoil as I sorted through what I knew and what was assailing my senses.

As we walked in step, horns blasted. Behind, sounds of bodies pushing through shrubbery and low hanging trees thudded. I whirled around and saw, dashing between the closely set trees, nightshades barreling toward us.

"The trees!" Temper hissed. "Climb now!"

I followed his advice and clambered up a thin oak as the nightshades sprinted past. The brown deceased foliage around me cracked as I placed hand or foot near it. Leaves fluttered aimlessly below, creating a brown snowfall. Safely perched on sturdy branches, Will and Katy eyed me worriedly. Temper inched his way as high as our tree went, before contenting himself to watch the gathering below us.

As we'd ascended, the horde of nightshades had run into the clearing before us. Sunken into the side of a small hill, a large flat obelisk hummed. I squinted as black shapes darted underneath me. One of the shapes, paler than the others, staggered under persuasion from whip and insult.

Tim, tired and defeated, stumbled over a protruding root.

The nightshade at his back snarled and cracked a long, leather whip over his head. I yearned to leap down and distract the nightshade but knew my arrival would only spell disaster for the others. Once revealed that humans sought shelter in the trees above, the nightshades would climb and retrieve all. I hooked one arm around a branch and leaned as far forward as I dared.

"Get up, you sniffling scum," the nightshade stalked forward. Tim stood, hands before him, and backed till he stood directly beneath me.

He didn't get an opportunity to make any of his momentary rest for the nightshade grabbed his collar and shoved him out into the clearing with the others. Rowdy and boisterous, the horde chanted and slammed spear against shield and sword against armor. The clearing and subsequent line of trees became filled with raucous jeering. I gritted my teeth.

The obelisk began to hum loudly, its only visible face glowing red before vanishing altogether—replaced with a black entrance, like an open doorway. From the blackness, a figure stepped forth. A human form made of smoke, it wore a black cloak and a single red hourglass had been imprinted on its chest. Where the head would have been, a solitary band of golden metal hung above the shoulders. Leather straps hung from its arms and legs.

Glancing out of the corner of my eye, I viewed Temper. His face had drained pale and his mouth had opened. His hairs stood on end and sweat glistened on his brow. Never before had I seen such terror in his eyes. It paralyzed him.

The form moved forward and laughed, the sound echoing in a series of increasing waves, like the ripples in a pond after a pebble is cast in. Those sounds seized control of my heart. It's hard to describe what one does not hear. Much like the language of the nightshade, one felt the laughter more than heard it as it reverberated through the valleys and mountains.

"Not possible," Temper shook his head, his eyes glued to the scene unfolding below. "It's simply not possible."

The form drew a sword made of smoke that deformed and formed again every time the wind changed intensity or direction. Once more, I felt the words bounce from the walls and enter my body.

"You stand before Gogothron, Second Hourglass to Mordën and Guardian of the Ninth Entrance to the Black Realm." The headache returned, and I kneaded my skull.

"We bring a prisoner," growled the nightshade, one of the companions of the boy." Seemingly unfazed at the arrival of Gogothron, the creature moved a step closer. "Let us pass. We bring tidings to the Widow which must reach his ears."

"Enter..." said Gogothron and then faded into the wind, the dark essence of his form dispersing and lifting off into the sky.

"We have to do something, now!" I hissed.

The nightshades began to march into the gaping hole, sheathing weapons. As they entered, I watched Tim forcibly shoved after them.

We waited in the trees for several minutes, breathless and fixated upon the humming obelisk. Realizing its purpose, I began to slide down the tree, careful to move slowly and purposefully.

"I'm going inside," I murmured back to the others. Temper stared down.

"Know that, if we go in there we may never return. Think carefully, Phoenix. I offered to take you as far as this general area. I do not lightly abandon you, should I do so, but what lies in wait, hidden in the dark corners of the belly of the earth is not something you could possibly imagine."

"Tim is down there," I said. I took one hesitant step toward the obelisk, conscious that at any moment a nightshade or worse would march into view. The cool morning air flowed through the clearing, sending the treetops swaying.

Will clambered down, followed by Katy. Last and most reluctant, Temper crept down the tree, his sword drawn and at the ready.

"If Tim is down there," I said, "my parents might be too. I don't ask any of you to continue with me. If any of you want to turn back, I won't blame you."

"You'd have a better chance at winning the lottery than

scaring us off," Will said.

"Yes," said Katy. "We are with you, Phoenix... till the end."

"Well then," said Temper, "look your last upon the natural light, for I fear we will go many days without it."

We moved toward the obelisk entrance and stepped inside. The sound of a sword being drawn from a sheath hissed in the darkness.

I froze.

6 · Death's Cold Embrace

Temper, already in motion, spun to face it. The soft breeze which moved from the outside and down into the festering tunnels below brought with it a rank smell that sent me reeling backward in moaning disgust. A nightshade appeared in the obelisk entrance, its shadow cast long and threatening over what light issued from the outside. In a fluid move, Temper dodged the creature's first jab and swung his sword.

The creature, snapping its pinchers aggressively, eyed us, and attempted to bypass Temper. It lost its head as Temper cried out and cleaved it from its shoulders. The creature let out a horrific shriek as its head rolled into the darkness. Before Temper had a chance to rest, more nightshades began to crowd the obelisk entrance, shouting and snarling.

"Run!" Temper roared. "Run for your lives!"

He bellowed as a dagger pierced his shoulder. A second dagger found its way into his stomach. Doubling over, he swung his sword wildly, doing his best to keep the advancing horde at bay.

"Down the tunnel!" Will cried—we turned to run, but I paused.

"We can't leave Temper," I argued.

"He can't hold them off forever," Will snapped. "If we are killed right here this was all for nothing."

Deeper in the tunnel, lit torches began to grow in intensity as their bearers rushed like madmen, shrieking and slamming shields against the walls. I glanced about wildly. We were trapped between an advancing nightshade force and Temper at the entrance to the tunnel.

"Down this side tunnel," Will called as he peered down a secondary tunnel.

"How do you know that's not the main tunnel, and—"

"Who cares?" Katy cried as we reached the gaping mouth.

I hesitated for a brief moment as time slowed. Thundering in rage, Temper backed further down the tunnel and swung his sword before him. He turned and gazed at me, barely registering as a sword drove into his side. A single tear fell from his eye as I silently thanked him. He smiled as the horde of nightshades piled on top of him, and he vanished beneath the black bodies.

Will yanked my arm and dragged me down the tunnel. Completely blinded, we staggered forward in uncertain strides. More than once, we cried out in pain, stumbling over a hidden rock or bouncing off a turn in the tunnel. Behind us, the stone walls caught the light of torches borne by nightshade berserkers.

"How come they don't just appear out of the shadows and end us?" Will ground his teeth. Breathing heavily, he blinked away what tears threatened to fall. "Can't they teleport?"

"Are you actually *wishing* for them to catch us?" Katy scolded as our arms were extended out and we probed forward as quickly as possible.

I swallowed as panic surged inside me. The fire grew closer as we became hindered in our flight.

"If we don't do something soon," I said, "we're dead."

We rushed around a bend and stopped. A cavern extended beyond our sight, melting into the darkness. Sconces dotted the walls, empty of their torches. Before us, eight tunnels branched off, two going up, two down, two to the left, and two curving right. Shouting came from four of the tunnels as various lights illuminated their dark winding halls.

"You two take one of the passages going right," Will glanced back. The nightshades chasing us were closing in.

"Don't be insane," I snapped as I moved to peer down each

tunnel mouth. "We go as a team. I absolutely refuse to—"

"I'm not leaving it up to you!" Will grabbed my shoulders and shoved me into one of the tunnels curving right. I cried out as I crashed into a stone and flopped to the ground, hidden by the dark shadows. Katy landed on top of me as the small room behind exploded with light. The nightshades following us flooded into the chamber, snarling and shrieking in deafening tones.

Will, caught like a deer in the headlights, turned and sprinted down a tunnel. The horde of creatures clambered after. I flattened myself against the stone, wrinkling my nose as the smell of unwashed bodies flooded past. Katy, petrified, remained motionless next to me. We pressed close together, and in any other circumstance, I would have blushed.

The room emptied quickly as the nightshades followed Will. A feeling of grief surged inside me as I wondered if I would ever see Will again.

"Will!" Katy wept bitterly. I coddled her close, feeling her warmth flowed over me. She shook as sobs racked her body. The sudden grief that I'd kept pent up inside flooded out as I remembered Temper's smile and Will's sacrifice. Somewhere, Tim and my parents knelt at the mercy of the Black Widow. We lay anguished and broken upon the cold stone.

▲▼▲▼▲

The darkness hung low, blanketing the blackened stone. Only the sound of his scratchy breathing filled the silence. A small pool of glistening water reflected his visage, and as he knelt his lip raised in repulsion. Raul raised a hand and placed it to his face. The uneven flesh blistered at the touch, rotten and splitting as his fingertips lightly brushed it. A single torch illuminated the chamber, casting an orange glow behind his head. With only the sound of his breath to mitigate his isolation, Raul sat. Waiting. A feverish desire to break free of the confines of the mountain tunnels tugged at his inner core.

"Come!"

The single word was magnified by his delicate hearing. Glancing once more at the black lines which crossed beneath his skin in swirling patterns, he stood. Only a humble tunic covered his shame as he blinked and ran a hand through his hair.

They were waiting for him. He stepped from the small chamber, escorted by a small unit of nightshade guards. Their polished black armor glistened, occasionally offering up eerie reflections of what he'd become. He winced at the bright light of the torches. Leather slid against leather and metal boots clanged against the unyielding floor. The torchlight flickered and cast their shadows in disproportionate swoops along the climbing walls. Raul *sensed* more than saw the swords and daggers held in his direction. Despite his years of unwavering service and loyalty to his dark liege, he'd still never trusted the creatures of the Pit—but now he had joined their ranks. He glanced at his hand and it seemed foreign to him. Much of his memory had been taken, like water being squeezed from a soaked sponge. Only information that his master deemed worthwhile remained at his disposal.

Raul opened his mouth to speak but found only guttural growls issuing forth. He cleared his throat, attempting to speak to those who surrounded him, but found himself unable. The closest shade, a burly guard with nine eyes—a rarity—clicked its pinchers together and glowered menacingly. The creature gestured with its long pike, and Raul raised his hands in mock surrender. He tried once more to speak but found words were a concept he could not seem to grasp. Much like his memory, his understanding of verbal communication, had abandoned him in favor of an undying loyalty he didn't understand.

He was escorted down various tunnels, some devoid of light, others were bathed in brilliant orange. Raul strained to peer into the dark places. When at last they broke through the confines of the tunnels, Raul welcomed the light with a smile and upturned head. The warmth of the torches returned. He stood at the edge of a bustling chamber, wider than it was tall. Its far walls lost to shadows.

Raul stood grimly, arms at his side as various nightshades dressed him. Old garb cast off and bared to the world, Raul gazed intently once more at his flesh. He felt unease. Leather was strapped to his arms, rough against his bare skin. A helmet of iron was placed over his head and as it settled into place, he felt its heavy weight burden him. An iron cuirass was strapped to his chest. A sword was placed in his hand, and at that moment, Raul felt formidable. Whatever past failures had led him here—he truly could not remember—were meaningless. Nothing could taint or diminish the power he now felt.

He turned and faced the creatures who had dressed him. They stared back in awe.

When he spoke, the words came easily, as though writ large in his mind by an unseen hand.

"Raul is no longer fit to be my title, for in his gracious will, the Widow has gifted me the new name of Hobbes. I shall be your commander, and together we will wipe out all those who oppose us, for too long have the Grey Cloaks and all who pledged fidelity to them plagued our perfect world of darkness with their tainted light. Today marks the beginning of their end, for we will issue forth and fear no death. Victory will be ours! For glory shall we blow the horn and shout the Black Widow's name amongst the cries of war! I charge you to fulfill your oath to he who blessed you with life!"

The nightshades in attendance roared their approval, slamming swords against shields and pikes against the stone. Pebbles rained from above as a nightshade stretched out its hands and gripped Raul's helmet. Raul lifted his head back and stared with hatred into the darkness of the ceiling. What wrongs had been done to the Widow would be avenged. He opened his mouth and bellowed. His cries of vengeance rang through every hall and shook every stone.

Death would come to the world beyond.

▲▽▲▽▲

The darkness suffocated me. I gasped for breath and silently pleaded to awake from the nightmare we found ourselves in. We'd lay grief-stricken on the tunnel floor, and it seemed as though time had stopped. That was dangerous. The shadows cast upon the walls by the torches in the main chamber had died down to smoldering embers, glowing spots in the darkness where light clung to life. I choked out a final shuddering breath, forcing myself to regain composure.

"We can't just leave him!" Katy wept. Tears flooded down her cheeks and splattered on the stone. "He was your friend! He was our friend!"

"Will's sacrifice won't be in vain," I whispered as I rose. "But now we have to keep moving. When they catch up to Will, they'll realize what he did and retrace their path till they end up here. We cannot allow ourselves to be captured. Hurry!"

We took hands and began to run quickly down the tunnel Will had shoved us into. A nagging feeling of doubt belied my feigned confidence. The concern and fear I felt for Will and Tim threatened to bring me to my knees. After a moment Katy pulled up.

"How can we continue?" she asked. "It's not just Will and Tim. Temper's lost too. This was a crazy idea from the start. How long before we're cornered and caught down here?"

She was scared, I could hear it in her voice.

"A crazy idea?" I let go of her hand. "I didn't ask for any of you to come along, Katy. In fact, I asked that you *didn't*, but we all agreed upon the risks and everyone understood the dangers we faced."

The look on her face was hurt and angry.

"To think I trusted you to lead us, to be there for us."

Katy's words sunk into my flesh and dug painfully.

"So, hang on, are you saying you don't trust me now?

The composure I had constructed had begun to shatter as I realized the implications of her words.

"I want to trust you, but how can I when..." She threw a hand to her mouth.

"When *what*, Katy?" It sounded angrier than I wanted.

"Tim and Will and Temper. They're gone. What happens when it's me, Phoenix? Are you just going to forge on ahead? Keep your eye on the prize?"

That stung.

"I didn't plan for any of this to happen," I retorted.

We'd come to a stop at a juncture which branched in two separate paths. Katy faced me—her face defiant with grief.

"No, you didn't, you're right. It's all on us. We're just collateral damage, I guess."

Tears trickled down her grimy face as torchlight lit her like a fever. I opened my mouth to speak but found no words. Katy wept.

"Look," I said wanting to reach out and hold her but not having the nerve, "we came *for my parents*. I came for them anyway, and you guys came with me. I'd have called it off, but how could I? Do you think it's not killing me what's happened? This has turned into a nightmare. But if we're caught now, it's all been for nothing. And that would be even worse. We just don't have time for grief right now, Katy. While we're free, there's a chance we can do something. But if we're caught..."

But Katy was backing away, shaking her head. She stared at me in a combination of pity and disdain and disbelief. A feeling of betrayal set in as I faced her.

"I loved you," she finally said, her eyes betraying her misery. "From the moment we set out, I couldn't deny my feelings, but now? I don't know anymore. I want to make you promise never to abandon me down here, but I don't want to put you in a position where you have lie."

"I love you!" I stepped forward and held my hands out in a gesture of peace. She backed away for a second time, increasing her distance. "Katy, I understand the pain and sorrow you're going through. I feel every ounce of it, whether you believe me or not, and it has snapped me inside. But we can't let it cripple us, or we're dead. Not just you and me, but Will and Tim and my parents, all of us. We're the only chance any of us have. You have to trust me."

"I'll follow you, but I can't trust you."

The statement sent shivers through me as her eyes filled with tears. I felt as if a knife had been plunged into my back and I was expected to continue. A hundred voices in my head each fought to be heard but the words were lost. All that remained was an indecipherable roar of pity, anger, self-recrimination, and regret.

I forced the tears back and nodded.

"I'm sorry," I murmured softly.

Katy turned away from and breathed heavily, removing all grief from her eyes and adopting a posture of neutrality.

"We need to hurry," she said, her voice sounding husky and strange. "The nightshades will return. We can't linger."

"Right," I said. "So let's—"

"Phoenix..." She'd back up into me. That's when I realized it hadn't been Katy who'd spoken.

Straining my eyes for any nightshades creeping along the walls, hidden in the shadows. I saw nothing but large grey outcrop of stone—*unusually* large.

The lump moved and a figure clad in grey loomed out of the darkness before me. I instinctively stood between the new arrival and Katy, throwing all concerns over our debate aside. Ducking momentarily, I grasped a loose stone and held it high, ready to cast it at the first sign of battle.

"And what will you do with that?" the smooth voice returned in mockery. "You would cave my skull in without giving me a chance to speak?"

"Who are you?" I demanded. I hoped the shake in my hand was not as noticeable as I felt.

The man laughed, and I paused for the laugh seemed to rekindle some lost joy.

"It is good to see your fury for the unknown burns bright." The figure stepped into the light, and I stepped back as the fire showed the features of a young man. His bearded face was partly shrouded by his grey cloak which he wore proudly over his broad shoulders. A bow was slung over his upper torso and a broadsword sheathed at his side. A quiver of arrows was strapped to his back over the cloak. He pulled the hood back and the light revealed his tan face. He glanced at me with a fatherly smile.

"Do you still deem me one of the minions of darkness?" he asked and laughed. His laugh was full of mirth and joy, and his face was pleasing to look upon. He placed his hand on the hilt of his broadsword. "My name is Quire, and I am at your service." He bowed deeply. "Before you worry, I do not consider myself employed nor tied to the Widow's demands. There are many who fight alongside you in your efforts to dethrone he who would see all crumble before him."

"How did you find us?" I challenged, hesitant to accept his explanation.

"You quite literally collapsed in front of me," he said with a shadow of a grin. "I was standing in this very place when I heard your approach and feared a patrol of nightshades had found me, so I hid. This cloak does wonders to redirect the eye's intensity. You could be standing but a nose away from me and mistake my garb for these monotonous stone walls. However, your words abolished any suspicion I might have harbored toward you. It is clear now to whom your loyalty lies."

"You could be trying to lure us into a trap." I narrowed my eyes. The rock in my hand began to feel heavy.

Quire chuckled and turned to Katy. "And you, fair maiden

of the golden hair, do you too believe my words carry the evil of the Widow?"

"You don't look like any we've seen so far," she said. "But if you're not then why are you here?"

"An astute observation and yet here you stand also." Quire released his hand from his sword's hilt and crossed his arms. "Should I deem you to be smaller versions of his spies?"

"We come to rescue of my parents," I said, "and two of my friends who journeyed with us."

"We had one more," Katy's voice dropped as she glanced quickly at me, "but he perished at the hands of a horde of nightshades."

"My condolences." Quire's face darkened with the revelation, and he inclined his head politely. "I also offer my regrets to your companions and their dreadful outcome. You'd do well to accept their fate, for none have escaped the Black Widow who fell into his grasp."

"My parents are strong." I lifted my chin. "They will have found a way to survive. All this misdirection still hasn't proven you are not a servant of the Widow."

"You desire a test?" Quire tilted his head.

He unsheathed a hidden dagger and handed it to me. Surprised, I gripped it and Quire knelt. He directed the cold steel and placed it against the softness of his flesh.

"If you trust me not, I shall impart to you my fate. If you deem me a shadow servant, end my life, for not one of those cursed beasts deserves to draw breath."

I gripped the dagger and watched the tip nicked Quire's skin. A single drop of blood appeared, but Quire remained steady, his face betraying nothing. The weapon hung in the air, pulling my hands closer to his neck as if guided by an unseen weight. I wrestled with the desire to protect Katy, a feeling that even now pained me, and to trust him.

"If you're deceiving us" –I lowered the blade and Quire sighed with relief– "you're convincing. You'll forgive our caution, but with all we've lost, I'd be a fool to abandon suspicion."

"You did what the situation demanded of you," Quire said. He retrieved the dagger and sheathed it, his cloak masking the sheath's location. "If I were in your place, I expect I'd do nothing less."

"What are you doing here?" Katy cleared her throat. We turned to look at her. "You act like you have no reason to distrust us, yet we have shown no love toward you. There's no reason for you to trust us unless you knew about us already."

I mentally chastised myself for overlooking her point. Quire gazed thoughtfully, rubbing his chin stubble.

"Quite so. As it turns out, I *have* heard of you," he confided. "to be truthful, you *are* the reason I am here."

I hastily stepped back, conscious of the weapons he could bring to bear at any moment. Fluidly, Quire raised his arms, hooking the edges of his cloak and pulling them back. In doing so, he revealed every object and weapon concealed beneath.

"Calm, my friends," Quire spoke carefully. "I swear this oath to you: I am no servant of shadow, and I have no fealty to him or his minions. I am Quire, Commander of the Grey Cloaks. We have had many interactions with Temper, and it is for him we come."

"Grey Cloaks?" Katy wrinkled her nose. "Temper? How do you know of him?"

"The Grey Cloaks are servants of the High King who dwelled once in the Citadel. Temper is our leader, and we recently lost contact with him. As per his instructions, we waited a full day, and now, I have come to retrieve him. I proceed my men. They wait on the hills to return with me."

I felt my throat close and a tear threaten to fall as I remembered Temper's slight smile to me as he fell to the tunnel floor, overwhelmed with black bodies stabbing and ripping at him in all methods of gory manner. I closed my eyes.

"Temper fell to a horde of nightshades not more than two hours ago. He gave his life so we could continue our quest. I'm sorry." The words scraped out of my throat and burned hotter than fire as they left my mouth. They snagged on my lips and did their best to hang firm. The simple act of speech had become a luxury and one which my own emotions seemed to deprive me.

"Dead?" Quire's demeanor shifted as he stared in cold disbelief. "You speak of Temper MacQuire? I pray you jest with me now. Friend, do not do me this dishonor after I have so openly brought you into my confidence." He pulled the cloak once more around himself.

"He is not lying," Katy glanced at me and in her single look I felt sympathy. "We entered the tunnels, but it was a trap. A horde of nightshades were waiting in the shadows and would have easily overwhelmed us all had Temper not used his own body to block them. He is the only reason you found us alive."

Quire dropped to one knee and breathed heavily. He looked up, and I recognized the agony on his face. His eyes filled with tears as he leaned against the wall.

"Temper was our leader." His words had dropped to a barely audible whisper as he placed a hand over his eyes. "He came with us on that fateful night. We were loyal."

Out of respect, I took a step toward him and awkwardly patted his shoulder. He wept bitterly. His trembles of agony wailed into the dark expanses of the tunnels, and for a moment, I felt the urge to weep with him. Temper had been more than a guide, more than a friend of Katy's. He had risked his life to bring us here, despite the dangers. His sacrifice and those of my friends brought me nothing but gut-wrenching guilt.

Quire dried his eyes and stood, his face red. "Friend, I thank you for delivering this to me. It is truly by fortune's fate that we have crossed paths even if it was for such a simple message. Temper was loved by all in my company, and his death will not go over well. He was a leader, a true warrior. His blood stains these cursed halls now, his final breath one separated from his friends and those who would weep at his passing. Oh for such times to be mine when the minstrel's voice sings no more and the warrior's steel is drenched in its bearer's blood."

I glanced at Katy. From her words about Temper, he'd been a known recluse and a potential criminal. Quire's description fit a different man altogether, a man who people could love.

"I must admit that comes as a surprise to me, Quire," I said. "You speak of a man I didn't know. Temper was a recluse in Clearwater, few knew him very well at all."

Quire gave a smile, almost identical to Temper's last. "Maybe one day we shall share the tale. In honor of his sacrifice. For now, allow me to take his place. Long have I studied the extensive tunnels beneath this mountain, and I believe my knowledge may come in handy."

"You are too kind," Katy said warily and shook her head at me. "And we are sorry for you loss, but now we really have to—"

"I know where the captives are held," he said.

I turned back to him.

"You can tell me where they might be keeping my parents? Hang on, how do you come to know that? If you were a friend of Temper and an enemy of the Widow then—"

"Study, as I say. One must know his enemies, and I have studied mine," he said. "You have only to bid me do so and I shall take you to your friends and parents, but we must move in haste." Quire ducked down the tunnel, keeping his cloak close at his sides. "As to further questions, I believe you stressed time is not on our side. Behold, our foe has found us."

Ahead a faint light kindled in the dark winding corridors. It grew in intensity, an orange glow bathing the stones in soft warmth. The torchbearers however were anything but warm as they stomped around in search. Far ahead, I heard the shouts and snarls of nightshades pouring through tunnels. Curses and bellows echoed down to us.

"They've found us!" Katy hissed.

"Follow me!" Quire bolted away, low and fast.

We sprinted behind him. The darkness once again enveloped us, broken only by the occasional torch. I'd already begun to yearn for a breeze, the kind that sweeps along a mountainside and flows out over the plains carrying the voices of birds and streams and life—voices lost to the stony silence of caves and tunnels. Festering filth resided here. Where once small animals called home, now looming beasts resided. I felt anger harden inside. The pain and grief which had tormented me now fueled the rage which had begun to inch its way throughout. Katy's words of betrayal echoed like the barks and bellows of nightshades in the caverns. I blinked back a tear and glanced at her. Silent at my side, she kept her focus ahead and followed Quire's every turn.

Quire—whose naked grief for Temper was what she had expected from me.

As we rounded a bend, Quire stopped. His sudden halt caused Katy to crash into him and I into her. She yelped and brushed the hair out of her eyes. I blinked rapidly, straining to see over her shoulder at the cause of our stop. Running toward us, swords drawn were two shrieking nightshades.

And Quire was gone.

I grabbed Katy and spun her around only to see a third Nightshade had come up behind us and was glaring at us with all eight of its eyes.

"He's abandoned us, Katy," I said. "But I won't. I promise. I love you."

Katy said nothing. She had the small silver knife that Temper had given her, and I grabbed mine.

The closest Nightshade roared, drew back its sword, and readied to bring it down on my head. In a single movement, a shadow detached from the wall beneath a sputtering torch and slashed at the creature. Howling in surprise, the Nightshade stumbled and collapsed. Its sword flew across the stone floor and came to rest at my feet. The shadow lifted the cloak around it and Quire stared back. I reached down, grasped the sword, and charged. His back to the second Shade, Quire failed to see the deadly arc before it had already begun. I screamed and jabbed my new weapon's point into the air behind Quire. The blade buried hilt deep into the surprised Nightshade. The creature's pincher clicked several times before it slumped to the floor.

Katy screamed as the third Nightshade grasped at her, its clawing hands gripping her neck. The creature drew a curved dagger and prepared to slash her throat. I heard a hiss and a smooth arrow appeared in the creature's back. I turned in alarm and raised my blade.

Standing in the middle of the tunnel stood Quire longbow in hand, a second arrow knocked.

Katy collapsed. The tunnel was silent. I went to her and helped her to her feet. When I turned around the bow was slung over Quire's shoulder again and he was nudging the corpse of the nightshade I'd killed.

"That was quick thinking on your part," he said. "I owe you my life."

"I just reacted without thinking," I muttered numbly. The sword in my hand seemed to grow in weight and I let it clatter noisily to the floor. "I've never... killed anything before."

"Remember the cardinal rule when engaging in combat with shades: do not grant mercy nor quarter for you shall receive none!" Quire flattened himself against the wall as a sudden torch appeared several hundred feet behind us.

We waited for the stomping and snarling to pass us by as the creatures of darkness howled in rage. Comrades dead and no signs of their fugitives, the Nightshades scrambled away in disarray. I peeked out from behind Quire's outstretched cloak.

"I do believe I trust you now," I grimaced as Quire stepped back.

"You asked for a test, and I delivered." Quire's eyes twinkled as he let slip a small smile.

"You said earlier you knew where our friends are being held," Katy spoke up.

Quire dashed down the tunnel after tunnel, and we followed. Turns and branches and junctions, more than either of us could hope keep track of at even half the speed. We were climbing at times, but more often descending. It was disorienting, and one thing become very clear.

We would never find our way out with him.

"Where exactly are you taking us?" I called out. I placed a hand against my side as a familiar throbbing pierced my stomach. All the years of donuts and pizza and choosing to study with Katy—instead of going to the gym with Tim—began to conspire against me. My muscles screamed in protest, threatening to seize should I continue to run without rest. The fire in my limbs sent abrasive shudders through my body. My vision whitened as spots danced before my eyes. All around torches and stone loomed out, mocking me. I swiped at what I thought was a leering Nightshade only to connect painfully with a protrusion of rock.

"We are heading to the lowest level," Quire said grimly. "We're going to hell."

7 · The Hadean March

"If we're going to be running like this for a while," I gasped, "perhaps we should get to know each other better. My name is Phoenix."

"Phoenix Rather and Katherine Chase," Quire let slip a second grin.

Unease joined the pain in my gut.

"You know us?" Katy jogged at his side, giving me a worried look. I shrugged.

"Not many who now live have heard anything but rumor of you," Quire ducked beneath a stone arch. "The tales don't do you justice." He glanced at me, sympathetically. "Although I believe they may have exaggerated, but what great lord doesn't welcome embellishment?"

"I think you have me confused with someone else," I slammed into a wall. "I'm no great lord, I'm a high school student, who finds himself caught up in something sinister and out of his depth."

"Ah," Quire nodded, "the mark of a true leader. Do not worry, most leaders are unaware of their future impact before it arrives."

"I said we should get to know each other, not confuse each other."

Quire laughed. "My apologies. As I've already told you, I am Quire, last Commander of the Grey Cloaks, and now your servant. Ask what you will of me, and I shall dutifully elaborate."

I staggered to a stop, heaving as I doubled over. Quire

slowed to a stop and eyed me. I waved a hand wildly.

"I just need to breathe." The pain in my side had grown and sweat drenched my clothes.

"We'll rest here," Quire said. "This is a little used tunnel. We shall be safe here. Sit."

I slid against the wall, collapsing in a pile of flesh and bones. Katy sat at my side and took my hand. Amidst the pain, I glanced at her. In our interactions with Quire, I'd forgotten our argument. She offered a smile and I returned it.

"Tell me about Grey Cloaks." I felt the pain subside and I could breathe again. Throat parched, I gazed at Quire. His demeanor had altered, and he stared doubtfully.

"Perhaps it's for another time," he held up both hands.

"No, I don't think so," I said with a smirk. "If you're really my servant, stop being evasive."

"Fair enough. Well, we are an old force," Quire's voice hushed. "We were created many millennia ago to serve as an elite corps of soldiers for the personal purpose of..."

He stopped and closed his eyes. Katy looked at me.

"If it's too painful," she said, "you don't have to explain it."

Quire nodded, and for a few moments, we sat in utter silence. After nothing but screaming and running to guide my thoughts for the last day, the stillness took on an eerie quality. The last torch in sight, a distant glow far off, illuminated our faces but not much else. All else was smothered in suffocating blackness. I glanced up and thought of the thousands of tons of stone just hanging over our heads.

"We must keep traveling." Quire shattered the moment, and I jumped. "We are not far now," he said.

The news lifted my spirits as I heaved myself up. Joints aching, I stretched. The tunnel emptied into a massive natural cavern. We followed him as he began to lead us along the lip of a deep ravine. The drop to one side grew steadily closer as the path narrowed. A moment before our own balance would have betrayed us and cast us into the ravine, the path widened, and we hurried out onto a smooth platform. A single roar echoed from the inky beyond and I stopped, fear seizing my limbs. The cry lingered in the air.

▲▼▲▼▲

Will gasped as the pain which raged inside him surged to a dizzying degree. Black spots dotted his vision. He coughed and felt blood trickle down his chin. The metal bed he lay on was cold to the touch and pitted with sharp spikes. Already he'd managed to tear his flesh on several. He glanced up through his agony and watched a face blur into focus. He blinked back the tears. Sweat moistened his face and dampened his hair.

"Who are you?" he moaned.

The effort to speak racked his body in a fit of painful contortions. The metal barbs, which had gouged his back, dug deeper. He coughed up a pool of blood and saliva and dangled his head to the side. The single torch in the room flickered.

"You are loyal and determined, William Gree," said the stranger. "Some might call you a true friend."

"Where am I?"

His throat burned. Will attempted to raise his hand to brush the sweat from his feverish flesh but stopped as he realized shackles chained him tightly to the table. He shifted his limbs and found them all to be chained tightly, allowing no room for wiggling. Only his head remained free to move around.

"Let us not concern ourselves with that just yet, my young friend. As to your first question, however, I am known as Raul."

Will was racked with wet coughs. The metallic taste in his mouth and the dizziness in his head sent his thoughts tumbling every which way. He attempted to pull a coherent idea out of his spiderweb of emotions.

"I need some water." His words felt thick in his tongue.

"I'm afraid I cannot give you any." Raul sounded genuinely regretful.

"What do you want from me?" Will whimpered. A ball of spittle dribbled down his chin. He slumped against the table, feeling the spikes sink incrementally deeper into his back. He moaned weakly.

Will couldn't help but yearn for relief from the agonizing pain of the torture bed. He felt the drops of blood trickle down the spikes and plop onto the stone bed. Every movement sent the spikes slightly deeper. He couldn't remember a time before the agony had invaded his limbs and the needle like stabs had pierced his every waking thought. He let out a scream as a curved hook caught the end of his feet. It tore deep into his flesh.

"What do you want?" he begged as the tears streamed down his ashen face.

"A nice blood meat," Raul mused as he withdrew the hook from Will's foot. He circled the bed, eying Will's body with a scientific interest. "Oh the possibilities if I had the time." He lifted the hook. Will noticed it was attached to a long metal pole, like a scythe.

Raul placed the weapon against the wall and stooped out of sight. Will wept bitterly and gnashed his teeth. Not one inch of his body didn't recoil with agony. He'd thought stepping onto a tack and seeing it sink deep into his foot had been the height of his pain. Now, as he lay, shaking and exposed, blood and the putrid odors of unwashed bodies assailing him, he cursed the day he'd been born. He cursed everyone he knew.

"If it's information you need," he finally managed to speak, "I know everything. I'll tell you whatever you need to know."

"Foolish one," Raul grimaced as he entered Will's limited vision. This time he held a long needle. Will glued his eyes to the device. "If information was what we desired from you, you would have spilled it all by now. No, you're are a worthless piece of the plan, and your time has come."

In a swift sure movement he jabbed the needle into Will's arm and, grinning, pushed the plunger down. Will stiffened as his arm began to burn. The needle appeared on the other side of his arm, pushing clear through the flesh. A red tinge framed Will's sight as he gasped and arched his back. A loud ear-piercing whine began to sound.

As if a blanket had been placed over him, the pain diminished. The roiling agony in his limbs melted away. His vision darkened. Or maybe it was the torch being put out. Darkness enveloped him and coddled him in whispering comfort. Only one painful reminder of his afflictions hounded his fading thought: a single burning sensation in his chest. Then all went quiet and he drifted off.

▲▼▲▼▲

I jolted to a stop as a second scream resounded off the cavern walls. It bounced and assailed my ears. Quire ducked his head and winced. The scream was not far off.

"Who was that?" Katy murmured. Her eyes had grown wide and she stared at me.

"Some unfortunate soul that has met his fate," Quire bowed his head. "We are reaching the lowest level. This is where the prisoners are kept. Do not let these noises disconcert you. Many find this their final resting place, loyal ally and foe alike, for the Widow does not discriminate as he plunges the dagger of death into them. He seeks only to destroy and corrupt those around him. We must focus on the task at hand and find your friends before all is lost."

Another scream from the darkness.

"Oh my gosh," Katy tugged at my hand, like an eager puppy receiving a tantalizing scent. "Phoenix, that was Tim. I recognize his voice. It—"

"Katy," I brought her close and stared into her eyes, "we both want to find them, but we have to brace ourselves for the possibility that—"

"No, shut up." Katy yanked herself free, glaring at me. "You may have given up," she hissed with surprising force, "but I will not. Tim and Will and the others are out there. The Phoenix I knew would rather die than entertain the thought."

She turned and began to move down the tunnel.

I stepped back as if a force pushed at me. A feeling of sadness draped over my shoulders, as if attempting to comfort me. Katy's words filled my head. Quire laid a sympathetic hand on my shoulder. I glanced up at him, forcing the tears back.

Quire lowered his voice. "Katy is a strong woman and in time, I fear, grief will tear her apart. She is right not to give up hope, but her own faithfulness will do her no favors here."

"What do you mean?" I asked softly as we followed Katy.

"The Widow bends even the strongest to his will, and in time he believes he will rule with an iron fist. I have known many great men fall under his spell and turn on their own brothers. You must be prepared to fight anyone." He leaned heavily on the last word, ensuring our eyes met. The torchlight on the walls flickered by some unseen force, and for the first time since entering the tunnels, I felt true fear.

"What are you saying?" My eyes widened.

"I do not mean to sow more fear where it already abounds." Quire shook his head. "Just be aware that not all you see down here may be what you desired."

Ahead, Katy ducked, her form vanishing into the darkness beneath the torchlight. We hurried up, low to the ground. She gestured for us to approach with silence as we ducked beneath a small torch and behind a pile of rubble. It was evident the stone wall had partially caved in and that the rubble we hid behind had once been the ceiling. Ahead, and nearly indiscernible amongst the various debris piles, two black forms stood motionless, their backs to a stone archway which led into pure blackness.

"Good eye," said Quire. He reached for his sword. "The real dilemma will be getting into the dungeon without alerting the guards and causing a commotion." The forms stood motionless and gave no sign they'd seen or heard us.

"I can distract them," Katy's had already started to stand when she spoke and neither Quire nor I reacted fast enough to stop her.

She strode in an alluring manner forward and out from the cover of darkness. The guards moved slightly to view her. For a moment no one made a move.

"Hello, um, boys..." Katy stopped several feet from them and cast her ponytail over one shoulder. She delicately placed one hand on her hip. I felt both disgusted and horrified as the scene unfolded. Katy flashed a brilliant smile. "Guard work must be routine and boring. You look like you could use a little uh entertainment." She reached slowly for the top of her shirt and in a blur of motion, both Nightshades drew their weapons and had placed them at her throat. She froze.

Quire leapt from the rubble, allowing his blade to shine in the fire. The orange flames reflected off the naked steel and bounced over the stone. In a single motion, both guards moved from Katy to let their blades rest threateningly off Quire's as he took a step back.

"We were made aware of your arrival," one guard snarled. The small pinchers protruding from his mouth snapped menacingly. "Drop your weapons and face the judgment of the Black Widow."

I felt around in the darkness, never taking my eyes off the guards. Quire stepped backward once more, eyeing the tips of the swords as they followed his every move.

"Gentlemen," he spoke cautiously, "I know how this may seem, but really I was just coming down here to bring you these children. I'm operating under the Widow's direct command."

One of the guards broke off as Katy began to move quickly toward the archway. He had her at blade tip before she'd made more than two steps.

"We were told there would be two children," said the guard

still on Quire. "But you are adult blood meat. Where is the other child?"

Quire swung his sword and beheaded both of the creatures with little effort. We hurried in to a room full of cells.

Each was crowded with people, all of whom wept with relief at our arrival. I glanced feverishly about, trying to find the source of the call, but the bodies which pressed the doors and called for aid drowned out my concentration and I felt the urge to scream. A horrible odor of feces and sweat assaulted my nostrils. From one cell, several teenage girls blinked at the bright light and reached out. They babbled about boys and a black car and how terrified they were. In the cell next to them a man more bones than muscle called.

"You must save me!" His shaky voice rose. "They plan to turn me into one of those monstrosities. You cannot let them! I'm a member of the Grey Cloaks. Please, have heart and let me out!"

Quire strode to the cell and in an instant gripped the hands of the man. His voice broke as he spoke softly to the prisoner. I stared into the faces of the captives. A rattling sound broke the tumult and all heads turned to the doorway. Quire stood, keys in hand, and rattled them once more for emphasis. From the cell closest to him, two elderly women moved slowly along, murmuring for help.

"Be still everyone and keep your voices hushed," Quire warned. "The Widow's minions still lurk in the shadows, best not alert them. Be quiet and all shall see the light yet."

He moved as rapidly as he dared. The keys jingled softly against the metal and even that small noise worried me. The shouts and cries died out, but their echoes still haunted the halls. As each cell door was opened, its occupants rushed out and hugged each other, letting their bony faces press against another's.

"Give me a key, anything," I hissed to Quire. He moved with haste yet was burdened down and his progress was tediously slow. He shook his head and gestured for me to post guard at the door. A large man, as far as I could tell the only well-fed man, stumbled from a cell and cursing, barreled for the door. I moved to intercept but he pushed past, and was lost to the darkness.

I moved stealthily to the door and peered into the shadows after him. My fears grew and I imagined fierce faces looming in the darkness, pale faces of horrific proportion. Spears bristled with the blood of my fallen friends and black eyes stared in haunted satisfaction. I wondered what would happen if a host of nightshades were to come marching down toward us. As far as my eye could perceive, the room that sheltered the captives had no exit save for the one we stood at. The chiseled stone at the back of the hallway held no small tunnels to escape into.

"Phoenix?" Quire's voice had changed from strained to hopeful as I turned around. "I think you'll want to see them yourself."

His simple words sent my heart clamoring as I peered into the dingy light provided by the single torch. Two faces moved toward me, and I placed my hand over my mouth as a gurgle caught in my throat. Hot tears welled up and spilled like ravaging waters over a dam. My limbs felt shaky and weak, and suddenly the very nature of our meeting and the place where we stood meant nothing to me. My father and mother hurried forward and embraced me, their eyes as red and wet as my own. For a few precious moments we trembled in each other's arms. I wept. The tears flowed with no end in sight as I let the tension and fear and pain and agony and depression collapse into a smoldering ruin of emotions. The grasp the Widow had had on me seemed to shatter and I could imagine a world where I could live a life of happiness. I barely noticed that my shirt had become soaked as I shakily stepped back. My mom held my head in her soft hands, her face beaming with sad joy. Dad, his face unusually grief-stricken, gave me a proud nod as he sniffed back the tears.

"Remain calm and quiet," Quire ordered as I opened my mouth to speak. The other captives around him quieted as a single man stepped forward.

"Thank you." A tall man stepped forward and addressed Quire. "I speak on behalf of the majority here. We were part of a hiking group that traversed the Pikes Peak trails. I extend my gratitude for saving our lives for we feared that we'd looked our last upon the sweet taste of freedom." He grasped both of Quire's arms and shook them. Quire returned the gesture.

"Do not thank me now," he said with a humble bow. "For your freedom is still unknown. Are you ready to move?"

The captives nodded, and Quire turned to face me. His face had relaxed into weary smile. We clasped forearms and for a moment, and he was about to speak when there appeared the harsh glare of torches coming down the tunnel beyond the archway.

"They've found us." Quire drew his blade and advanced swiftly to the doorway, peering out.

"You must take the captives and go," I said as I realized my final duty.

"What are you talking about?" Quire demanded as he gazed over the silent captives. "We move out as a group. I'm sure this horde ahead is no more trained than the first."

I laid a hand on his arm and he turned, a confused look on his face. The moment with my parents had revealed one sharp reality.

"I cannot lose my parents again." I forced the quiver in my voice back down. "It would be unbearable, not when we've come so far. You know these tunnels. You brought us here so I know you can take them out. And you must have found a way inside the mountain so it follows you can get back there. I am a blind mouse in a maze. I would lead them straight to the Widow himself before I led them to safety."

"I am honored to be at this reunion, Phoenix, but your first duty is to help these captives escape this place," Quire looked at me. "I can help you with that, but our window of escape is closing quickly."

"Go," I smiled at him. The advancing light revealed the chiseled, black faces of the spider heads. Quire, his eyes wide as he came to the same realization as I had, he turned to me.

"Humans have long since been held in ill repute for actions of ages past," He smiled, and for the first time, a single tear escaped and trickled down his grimy cheek. "If my forefathers could see you now, they would embrace you as kin. Farewell, noble Phoenix, may our light shine together in days to come!"

"Swear to me that you will see my family and these captives safely to the surface and away from harm. Swear it by your life."

The sounds of the boots against the stone floor thudded down with an ominous dark chant. The light grew close and I could see the eight individual eyes on each creature's head.

"I swear by the noble blood that flows inside me and by the power I wield with Ithënuil, my blade, to defend to my dying breath those you've entrusted to me," Quire inhaled shakily. He drew the blade and for a moment appeared to debate over giving it to me or keeping it.

"I accept your oath and, in return, promise to give you the time you need to help them escape," I swallowed. "Keep your sword, for it will do me no good. You may still benefit from its presence. A sword would do no difference in my inexperienced hands."

"Will you not reconsider and allow me to defend your escape?" Quire whispered in a frantic last attempt. The approaching creatures were a dozen seconds from arriving.

"They have a better chance with your knowledge to escape these cursed halls," I shoved him toward a small offshoot of the main tunnel, and the captives began to flood toward it, panicked at the approach of their captors.

Katy was swept along, her eyes wide with terror as she stretched out a hand and grasped my fingers.

"Come with us," she pleaded, her words full of fear. "You

can't stay. I love you. I can't endure this pain again. Do not make me feel this hurt anymore! I lost so much. I cannot lose you too!"

"Run, my Katy, run with the strength of a thousand men!" I returned, as our touch broke and she was forced down the hall.

"You truly are the one we've been looking for. Godspeed, Phoenix!" Quire turned and, sword in hand, followed the last captive down the black tunnel. His words echoed in my head as I turned to face the horde of Shades.

They came to a silent halt. I displayed my hands. In both, a jagged stone rested neatly. The creatures laughed and jeered as several of their ranks advanced with extended swords. Another group, armed with bows, readied to fill my body with their deadly darts.

I cast the first stone and watched as it bounced off a small shield held by the closest shade. The second stone followed quickly after, it too bouncing with no indication of pain off the shield. I backed away as taunts and jeers began to overwhelm me. Hands reached for me, and faces loomed out of the shadows, their pinchers opening wide as if to consume my face in their iron-like bite. I backed into the cell area and dodged the first grasps, letting the creatures snarl over their failure. Stones flew into their many eyes as I scrabbled about for any weapons. One reached for me and I kicked away his hand, only to feel a cold hand grasp my ankle and yank me to the floor.

It didn't take long for my hands to find themselves bound tightly and for my legs to be roped together with thick chains. I was heaved over the shoulder of a burly guard and they began to race back the way we'd come.

"Leave the vermin," one ordered as the horde turned and began to race back down the tunnel. "Our shades will hunt them down. We bring our prize directly to Raul."

"You idiot," a smaller voice snapped, "we bring the bairn to the Widow."

"Keep your mouth shut," the first voice returned.

The darkness pressed down around, broken only by the sparse torch whose light illuminated a few feet in front of us. The Shades moved wordlessly with clear intent. Only the sound of their feet slapping the stone convinced me the world had not been muted. I moved my lips, conscious of the tight gag which had been hastily tied. I bounced unevenly, like a sack of potatoes. My thoughts turned to Quire and my silent hope for his escape. I'd put my family's fate and the lives of all involved into his hands. My stomach churned at the forgotten farewell with Katy. I envisioned her wide eyes as she mouthed words which seemed alien to me. Ahead the passage forked, and without a moment's pause, the band of creatures turned right. The path dove deeper into the mountain, and the ceiling descended till my back nearly brushed its hard surface.

I was jolted as the creature carrying me leapt down a ledge and landed hard on a stone floor several feet below. My breath temporarily gone, I gasped. The creature looked up at me, and it's eight eyes seemed to soak up my pain with an eager obsession. We'd landed in what appeared to be a wide space with the occasional meandering tunnel winding out of sight into the bedrock.

"Place him in here!" a Nightshade growled as it drew its sword and gestured for my bearer to let me down.

I was dropped crudely to the floor and moaned. A Shade reached forward and yanked me to my feet. In a single moment, the creature's sword pommel collided with my stomach, and I bent over. A second blow sent me reeling back to the ground. A third slammed into my face, and I tasted blood as the harsh light from the torches began to fade. A fist connected with my chest, and I felt a crack. Vomit gushed from my mouth. A dagger slashed at my face and I felt hot blood run down my temple and into my eye. As my vision faded, and I slipped into oblivion, a face moved from the shadows and gazed down at me.

8 ‧ Mind Games

I awoke to gut-wrenching agony and threw up what little stomach contents I still had. The moist particles flew out of sight, and I arched my back, hacking and spluttering. My head pounded as if a hundred rocks pelted against it.

"So you are the bairn?"

The voice was barely discernible above my noisy coughs. I relaxed my body, shaking my head to distract myself from the pain. A single torch lit a small room and revealed a small mousy man. The man stepped forward and displayed his hands in a peaceful gesture.

"Can you hear me, young bairn?" The man inquired as he moved closer and peered at me.

I opened my mouth and forced out a guttural groan. The pain squeezed at my throat, and my eyes rolled back in my head. I arched my back once more and for the first time realized I'd been cuffed, wrists and ankles, to the platform I lay on.

"Ahhh, you can, and so soon." The man withdrew from my line of sight. "My name is Raul. You need no greeting for your name is the bane to which my master yearns. The blood which runs through you and even now is spilled for our glorious cause is his elixir. Tell me, what brings you into the spider's web? Does your own self-preservation have no say in your life? Surely, you know it was a mistake to seek out the victims of The Black Widow's ventures?"

"What did you do to me?" I finally spoke, my words like metal scraping across gravel. My throat burned and I squeezed my eyes shut.

"I believe the brutes outside fell to their instincts. I do apologize," said Raul as he moved around me. "They're primordial creatures, so I do hope you excuse their lack of manners. We were told to bring you unharmed, and as you can see, we've handled that particular mission splendidly thus far." He chuckled again and raised a thin wooden spike. The end dripped with a thick liquid. I eyed it.

"Let me go," I muttered weakly. I struggled to force the chains off my arms but, inevitably, crashed back against the platform.

"Oh I wouldn't struggle," Raul admonished, "the bed you lie on is already doing more damage than I'd hoped. Do keep still or the master won't have much left to interrogate."

For the first time I felt the wetness against my back and strained to see what liquid I lay upon. I realized where the pain stemmed from and screamed. Beneath me, barbed hooks dug into my back, tearing flesh and releasing blood. Every minuscule movement tore deeper into my back.

"What am I laying on?" A surge of strength returned and with a burst of energy I heaved upward. The chains strained and for a brief moment Raul appeared concerned.

"Now now, bairn," he snarleed and his brow furrowed with disappointment, "you are making a right mess of things." He lowered the stake and began to check that my chains remained secure.

As I lay, feeble and stretched like a man about to be torn in two, I heard a far-off tone. At first, in my delirium, I thought it was the trumpet of an angel come to bear me home. As the sound grew louder, Raul reappeared. He too paused and tilted his head to listen. The sound echoed once more, and I realized it as a horn. Outside the chamber, Nightshades rushed past in full armor. They morphed into the shadows and were gone.

"What's going on?" Raul called as a Shade appeared

in the doorway. The creature spoke in a language that sent goosebumps along my arms. The scratchy whine of its tone colored Raul's face ashen.

"It's too soon," he shook his head. "I have not yet even begun. The bairn is not ready. Tell our master the bairn is not yet prepared for him."

The creature snarled and vanished from view. For a third time, horns echoed in the deep. Their terrible cries sent the stone beneath me quavering.

"What's happening?" I coughed.
"It's none of your concern." Raul swept a set of crude looking devices into a black bag. "This is incredibly rude of me, and I apologize for this interruption. I was looking forward to working with you. Stay here until I return!" He hurried from the room.

"Of course, I'll stay here," I winced, "it's not like I had any plans today."

Time began to stretch, and the pain diminished as my body wore itself out. Even the slow extension of an arm or movement of my back caused no pain. My body had simply stopped feeling. As the darkness flickered around me and the sounds of rushing steps faded into silence, I began to take note of the room I lay in. I gazed upward. Statues lined the ceiling with faces distorted in anguish. Carved figures of noble warriors bore grimaces, and all save for one—who floated at the cavern peak—had their hands out in front of them, as though to ward off attack. Beneath the highest statues, paintings of women and children and livestock had been drawn to appear as if they were fleeing from some great evil.

The more I looked the more I realized that what I'd thought was the torchlight reflecting off of the stone was actually orange and red paints in fantastical sweeps and curls. A village or town was on fire and the warriors above fell before the onslaught of an unseen foe. Even their king had been slain. Fire ravaged the village, and women and livestock fled in fear of death. Golden flames licked at the edges of homes, and a wave of silent evil poured forth like a tsunami upon the populated rural scene.

I imagined the carnage which stretched from the coasts to the islands and the inner hearts of the lands. I envisioned countries toppling and banners of blood raised in their stead. Happiness and joy and love fled before the violent emotion of fear. I feared what would become of home and Colorado and my family should the Black Widow take control. Death and carnage would overrun all if his strength solidified. And as I pondered these things, an image formed in my mind: a far-off place, older and more precious to him and any depicted here.

I shut my eyes and could see a place of golden meadows and thriving cities of monstrous proportions. Spires and halls of stone and marble extended like jutting statements into the sky, a shield against his advancements. Long had this battle been waged and many were those he had subjugated to his will. Death was all that would await those who opposed him. Death was our future.

I opened my eyes and stared up once more at the grim scene above. I did not want this to be my future. I did not want to serve the Widow. I wanted peace.

Soon, my child, you shall see true peace!

The thought was not my own, and I threw my body against the table with force as I repelled the intrusive moment. It was as if a hand had penetrated into my head and planted the thought. I groaned and clenched my eyes shut.

Bow down before me and swear your oath, my bairn, and all this suffering shall be taken from you. I shall end your pain and release you.

The voice whispered into one ear and snaked out the other. Tears flooded down my cheeks, and I struggled against my bonds with a ferocity I'd not known I was capable of. My sweat stuck to the table. The cavern had begun to change and became as one moving organism. The stone rippled in undulating waves as small black orbs dotted the ceiling. Voices echoed in commanding tones and I screamed, wrenching my body up as I strained against the chains. My muscles bulged and my face grew hot and red as I collapsed back against the table.

The stone now beat like a heart, and the statues above laughed in cruel chorus as they rotated to peer down with lifeless eyes. Orange light flickered as flames approached, flames never ceasing and devouring everything in their path. I wept and gnashed my teeth as hundreds of horrific voices assaulted my mind, tore at my restraint, and battered my resolve. My very identity was pulled at, and in a single moment...

It all ceased.

The stone grew hard and cold and unmoving. The statues once more adopted their poses, and the fires diminished to flickering torchlight. Drenched in sweat, I lay defeated as my heart throbbed. My hair pressed down upon my brow and my eyes burned. I shivered and sweated simultaneously. All had been open wide before the forces of evil. I shut my eyes. All dissolved as thought and mind and being became weary of existence and faded away.

My body became lifeless and I drifted off.

▲▼▲▼▲

When I awoke, my throat was parched. The sounds within and beyond the chamber had since fallen quiet and the silence was near absolute. The torchlight had mostly gone out, and darkness now suffocated me.

A shadow moved. I wasn't sure how I even saw it move so dim was the light. It was almost as if I'd felt the form standing over me, powerful and prideful.

"Who's there?" I managed to say. My voice felt like sandpaper over rough wood. I coughed. The blackness made no response though the presence had become more real, gathering in the shadows. The utter solitude pressed down, as if hundreds of hands moved to crush the life from me. I gasped and for the first time noticed a small mote of light, no larger than a speck of dust.

It shimmered and grew. Light without source. Expanding until it threatened to envelope me. Then with a jolting suddenness...

▲▾▲▾▲

I stood in a courtyard.

The cobblestone yard sat between two blue ponds with bright green foliage on all sides. In the middle of the courtyard, lounging without a care in the world, a young man mused at the wonders of the world. He was visited twice by a young woman who vied for his attention but when he failed to even so much as look at her, she hurried off. As I gazed, I realized that whatever I was witnessing, it was not a place I was familiar with. The girl had worn a long flowing dress made of silk and precious fabrics. The young man, head in hand, sported a tunic over a simple grey shirt and rough pants. His black boots were caked in mud. He stood.

"I know you're there," he spoke with a pouting tone in his voice. Behind him the bushes shuddered as a slender figure stepped into view. He was masked by a deep cloak, the hood of which hung low over the figure's eyes.

"Pardon me, my liege," the form's voice was silky smooth, "but you did request that the information be fully validated before I come to you."

"And here you are, teacher," the boy yawned as if the conversation tired him. "What have you to report? Are the rumors true? Has my father perished on the battlefield?"

The figure reached up and with a fluid movement, removed the hood and let it fall softly against his back. He looked up and right into my eyes. I cried out as I realized his eyes were pure black.

▲▼▲▼▲

I gasped as the courtyard vanished, and I was once again stuck on the table, lost to the world in the forgotten tunnels the Widow had found and made his lair. It took me several moments to realize the pressure on my face. What felt like a gloved hand pressed down on my nose. I attempted to struggle, but I was spent. The mote of light reappeared...

▲▼▲▼▲

I stood atop a marvelous mountain and below me were spread the splendors of the world.

I stared around and marveled at the forest greens, ocean blues, sunset reds, and snow white which dotted the landscape below. In the distance, I could faintly see a city. Again, it was unlike any city I'd ever witnessed for instead of skyscrapers and the curling blanket of smog, a tall wall encircled and protected. The tallest structure appeared to be a single enormous obelisk, jutting into the sky with a demanding presence. I turned ever so slightly and jerked back instinctively as the same slim, robed figure stood at my side. He turned and once more displayed his pure black eyes. I fought the urge to scream.

"Who are you?" I demanded.

The figure turned and began to walk down the mountainside. Animals of a sort I'd never seen before fled in various directions at the man's approach. I noted with slight apprehension that grass and foliage touched by his cape, withered to a muddy brown. I hurried after him, and when I'd caught up, I reached out to grasp his mantle.

The mountainside spun away, and darkness replaced the great beauty.

This time, I was quicker to my senses and began to toss my head back and forth, aware of the heavy weight of the glove on my face. Above me, I could faintly make out a spot which was darker than the darkness, almost blacker than the surrounding void. The mote of light appeared for a third time...

This time, to my horror, I stood above a fiery pit which spanned hundreds of yards in diameter. A combination of mud and flames boiled into a hot froth as onlookers jeered and many shouted in a tongue I didn't understand. The same slim figure stood at my side, silent. His hood covered even his chin. I reached out and grasped for the fabric, but my hand passed through him. He turned to me, and I took a step back. Across the pit, a black-robed figure with a red hourglass painted onto his pale forehead stood and began chanting. Three other equally darkly clothed figures joined in—their combined voices carrying even to my ears.

"What are they saying?" I muttered.

"Ash, murk, death, violence, darkness, doom," said the figure beside me. The voices chanted and I felt goosebumps race down my arms and legs.

A figure in a white robe was shoved off the edge of the pit and, with a horrible scream, fell in. I gasped and my hand flew to my mouth. The action had happened so quickly.

"Watch."

The voice was abrupt. At my side, the figure pointed a long arm at the spot in the soup where the man had fallen.

I peered intently, hesitant of what I might see. The white robe floated unburnt atop the burning contents of the pit. The form which it had once clad, however, rose from the fire and mud. I wrinkled my nose as the naked figure stood tall. Its face had become blackened and terrible. I felt a hand on my wrist...

And suddenly I lay, heaving, on the table.

"What do you want from me?" I coughed. The darker blackness shifted, and for a moment I wondered if it was laughing. I saw the orange light a moment before, as I muttered a curse, I was gone from the room.

Before I even looked at where'd I'd landed, I gazed about for the slim figure who had accompanied me thus far. True to his past actions, he remained at my side.

"What is this?" I demanded, feeling curiosity overtake the fear. "I know this isn't real. None of this is real. I'm dying back in the Widow's lair. What do you want with me?"

"Look." The figure pointed and I turned, half expecting to see a man getting decapitated or a starstruck lover reciting a poem for his hidden love.

Bound with more chains and locks than I could count, a hunched figure sat crumpled, defeated at the center of a wide pavilion. Thousands of onlookers watched as he was held motionless by the weight of his chains. Not a person uttered a sound as a soft wind blew through the buildings around. I now knew I wasn't anywhere I'd been before. The homes were sculpted of ivory and wood. The road was paved with marble, and on every corner of every street, a tall curved pole with a torch on top illuminated every nook and cranny. Beyond the homes, the white obelisk I'd seen previously stretched impossibly high into the night sky.

"What is this place?" I murmured to my companion. He made no response but merely pointed again at the prone figure in the center of the pavilion.

"You have been sentenced with treason against the very creation which formed you, Mordën, blackest of souls!" The voice boomed from a dais and I gazed up.

Atop a thick wooden chair, a man in a white gown and flowing red cloak sat. His voice carried with curious ease over the heads of eager listeners. Voices murmured as the crowd of onlookers stirred. The man in the center of the pavilion shifted slightly, daring to look up toward the speaker.

"If you think you are free from the bonds of slavery..." the bound figure of Mordën began, but the rest of his response was lost to the jeering of the onlookers.

"You stand against god and man, against Ëonian and the Maker of All. By the blood of those you have spilt, we find you guilty of all charged against you. By command of the High King, you are to be banned from Ëonia without means of return."

Mordën laughed maniacally as if possessed by a devious spirit. He raised his head and, with great strength, fought against the weight of his bonds and stood. A tall man, even in his chains, he surveyed the watchful eyes of the gathered crowd.

"You think banishment will keep darkness away? Light cannot survive without darkness. You all will one day perish at the hands of the banished." He turned to the dais. "And you, High King, will you commit to this action and deny your god what is his due? You have only delayed the inevitable. I will return, and with vengeance tenfold will you face your punishment." He turned then to the crowd. "Your High King would act on your behalf, but let it be known his own actions have sealed your fate and the fate of generations to come."

"I know the price for which I speak," the High King stood. He beckoned away the advisory which hurried to his side. I watched with interest. Mordën gazed at him.

"You would accept the consequence of your actions against me this day, High King?"

"Mordën," he said, "I speak on behalf of all the free peoples."

▲▼▲▼▲

Without warning, the darkness returned. I felt sweat running down my face and chest. My muscles quavered as if I'd run beyond the point of exhaustion. My head pounded, and I had the metallic taste of blood in my mouth. I gazed up in dazed pain.

"The visions you see are remnants of a time long ago." I recognized the voice of the slim figure from my visions.

"Who are you?" I asked, repulsion creeping into my voice. "What do you want with me?"

The light returned as fire rekindled in the torch. The soft orange light slowly grew until the statues above began to shimmer into view and the roughhewn walls of the chamber began to show their uneven edges. I closed my eyes and silently begged to be alone. The horrors and grief and danger weighed on me like a millstone around my neck. Standing at one side of my platform, a tale thin man in a black suit stared down. His face was pale as snow, his eyes black as night.

"Greetings, bairn." He spoke softly, his hand running over my brow.

"My name is Phoenix." I forced the words out as I recoiled from his touch. "Why do you keep calling me bairn?"

I shrunk from his cold fingers, and for a moment he smiled. I never realized before how much I'd come to rely on the understanding of an individual's intentions based on the expressions through their eyes before. The pure black orbs, set deep into his pale skull, betrayed nothing. His crisp black suit was perfect, not even a speck of dust or ash marred his lapels. It was as if he were a freshly cleaned corpse taken from a casket and reanimated. His skin seemed stretched over his bony form, and his clumps of wispy black hair were held together by the scent of some unknown perfume. His nails were smoothed and fingers unblemished. As I looked up at his face a scream began to bubble up. I couldn't explain it, but

I felt the urge to throw up with revulsion.

"You are revolted by my appearance?" The figure stroked his jawline and his eyes seemed to pierce my very soul.

My breathing was heavy. "I don't know who you are, but I am not afraid of you."

"I never mentioned anything about fear." The man leaned over me and he grinned. His thin lips pulled back to reveal pointed teeth. "Tell me, are you terrified of me?"

I squirmed. "I came to rescue my parents. Whoever you are, I mean you no harm. What is your name."

"I see your sense of humor has not perished. I was once known as Mordën." He smiled and his pearly white teeth reflected the light.

"Mordën, like the man in that vision?" I tilted my head, a shred of curiosity overcoming my fear.

"I am known by that name and another." He raised his head and he grinned from ear to ear, a monstrous hideous sneer. The skin around his chin stretched and tore, the largest flap of flesh revealing bloodless gums and dried bone. I screamed and my eyes rolled back in my head.

▲▼▲▼▲

Quire watched breathlessly as the stream of captives ducked beneath the waterfall and rushed out into the wide-open space before the tunnel entrance. His brow furrowed, he sighed with relief as the forty-ninth individual stumbled into the blinding light. He hurried after them, ensuring the stone to the tunnel had been returned.

"You're late!" The voice was full of mirth as Quire whipped around.

"Thornburg!" He cried, his eyes lighting with joy. "My comrade!"

He embraced the tall man. They pulled back, and Thornburg gripped his forearms. They stared at each other for a moment before Quire, in his concern, turned away.

"Quire…" Thornburg's concern could not be hidden. "You've been gone over a fortnight. The men had given you up for lost. What happened down there? You clearly brought more than you went in with."

"They're captives from the deepest cells," Quire explained in haste as he hurried down the grassy knoll to where a band of men in grey leather herded the captives down the hillside.

"Captives?" Thornburg gripped Quire's arm, stopping him in his tracks. "Quire, you've been gone for two and a half weeks. You told us to expect you the next day. What happened to you?"

"I met him." Quire stared back. His voice was strained. "I met the bairn. He's down there, Thornburg. He told me, things."

"What?" Thornburg let his hand drop to his sword hilt. "What did he tell you?" His eyes narrowed.

"Not now," Quire shook his head. "We need to get these poor people away from here. The Shades are on the move. The Black Widow is planning something. Are the Grey Cloaks assembled like I asked?"

"They've been assembled these last several weeks." Thornburg's voice had shifted from friendly to professional as he began directing the men below. "We await your command."

Quire turned, his voice caught in his throat, and for a moment he said nothing.

"Quire!" Thornburg roared as he drew his sword and slashed at a spot behind Quire.

Quire whirled about, his own blade drawn as he instinctively deflected the sudden attack.

Nightshades, dozens, poured from the tunnel entrance. Their long, curved spears and red feathered arrows clashed with the splashing froth of the waterfall. Water sprayed into the air as a rainbow shimmered into view.

"We're outnumbered!" Quire dodged a spear thrust and swung his sword at the unprotected shaft. The spear splintered in two and the Nightshade holding it cast it to the ground.

It drew a blade and rushed, its mouth wide and its pinchers snapping open and shut with an animalistic ferocity.

Quire and Thornburg rushed down the hill as Nightshades shimmered into view from the shadows. The initial dozen morphed into a hundred. That hundred multiplied into a thousand.

"Run!" Thornburg bellowed as he leapt over a fallen tree. His nimble legs cleared the wood as he ducked and rolled into a ball. Several arrows sunk into the moist dirt around him. He brushed his hair from his eyes and beckoned for the captives and soldiers ahead to keep running.

A white sheen seemed to descend on the area as Quire turned and, in a split second, deflected an arrow which would have otherwise penetrated his skull. The black arrow broke in half, the red of the feathers brushing against his cheek as they flew off into the brush. He watched as several Grey Cloaks, their swords drawn, cried as they ran past him, toward the charging force. He turned and, ears ringing with the din of screams and battle, staggered along. He closed his eyes as he heard the sounds of metal slicing through flesh behind him.

"You have to get them to safety!" Thornburg rushed past him, his sword readied. "I'll hold them off. Get to the outpost! They're waiting for you. Tell them the three hundred stood their last."

He turned to the Grey Cloaks then, rallying them from retreat.

"To me! To me!" A black tidal wave of shrieking shades rolled down and over them.

Quire cried out as an arrow pierced his calf. He fell, rolling down the hill. Nettles and dirt rolled with him and over him and inside his clothing. The arrow broke off under his weight as he rolled to a stop. A horn shattered his hearing and the full sound of battle resumed in horrific intensity. Men screamed, metal clashed, and Nightshades shrieked in their foul tongue.

"Come!" A Grey Cloak reached down and helped him to his feet.

They hurried down the incline as the screeches and howls of shades grew closer. Behind him, a black wave of gnashing teeth and outstretched swords rushed toward him. Quire pushed off his escort and turned.

"Commander?" The man began to back away as he eyed the oncoming horde.

"Go," Quire spoke softly. He felt empty. The strength of his will had waned, and a dark cloud hung over his heart. The tidal wave of black rushed over him, dozens of swords and spears piercing his body as hands reached out and tore at his hair and flesh.

▲▼▲▼▲

My body was overcome with shivers as the chamber faded into view. Mordën stood over me once more, his hand placed on my face. I shook my head violently. The hanging flap of skin on his face didn't even faze me anymore. The exposed bone barely registered in my thoughts.

"What did you show me that for?" I cried bitterly. Quire's last look had been one of a man who'd lost all hope.

"I showed you the real enemy," he responded evenly. "You came to save your friends, an admirable intention. However, the world is no friend to life. You believe the Black Widow to be the source of your problems."

"He kidnapped my parents," I gagged.

"Death is your enemy," he returned. "Death ended the lives of those who came with you. The horde of nightshades ripped apart your friends and family. You are alone and without a cause."

I shifted, feeling the hooks beneath me tear open new areas of my back. I felt the blood drip down. The sudden realization of my family's death hit me like a punch to the face.

"They're gone?" I was barely able to force the words beyond my lips. My mom's face shimmered into view in my thoughts and I yearned to see her, to see my father.

"You must join me…" Mordën leaned down. His body reeked of embalming fluids and the soft dusting of makeup on his face shown in the light. "Together we can defeat our common enemy. Let me inhabit your body, your thoughts, and together as one we will return the world to a place free from death."

"Work with you?" I bit out. "You're the reason I'm here. You talk of death like a common enemy but your loyalty seems to lie with those who deal it. As for inhabiting my body I don't know what your…"

But he had stretched out his hand and my nose flared as I realized his intentions.

▲▼▲▼▲

I found myself standing in an old church, the pews full of members clothed in black. A strange white sheen seemed to cover the scene. At the front, by the altar, two oak caskets sat on a pedestal. I stared about, and an urge overwhelming feeling of nervousness swept over me. The faces of the grieving were downcast in some unspoken prayer as orange light glowed through the mosaics of colored glass along the walls. The atmosphere was reverent, as if a single motion would disturb the peace and the deceased would return in vengeance. A man in a black gown ascended the stairs and stood next to the caskets, running a worn hand over each. He sighed and turned.

"We are gathered here today to mourn the dear loss of Ted Andrew Rather and Ashley Elizabeth Rather…" The minister's voice boomed loudly across the pews.

For a moment I figured I'd heard wrong and looked about to see if I could identify who lay in eternal slumber. My eyes were drawn to a single picture on an easel. The blood drained from my face and black spots raced across my vision. I felt lightheaded.

My eyes narrowed as I stared in absolute horror at the caskets. A feeling of disbelief and grief flooded over me like a tidal wave over a helpless fishing village, and without thinking, without allowing my better half to take command, I screamed. The sound of pure grief which issued from my mouth flooded the church from corner to corner, and even as the minister spoke his horrible words, my cry drowned out his voice. Tears flooded down my cheeks, and I curled my fists into balls.

"How could you? How could you take them?" I held nothing back as spittle flew from my trembling lips. My body shook with sobs as I dropped to both knees. I opened my mouth again but this time nothing came out, just muted anguish beneath bloodshot eyes. Snot ballooned from my nostril and drool pooled down my mouth as my face grew splotches of red. Blood veins bulged in my neck. I collapsed.

▲▼▲▼▲

The cavern had returned, and I opened my eyes, tears streaming down my face. The intensity of the moment left me shocked, and for several ragged breaths I said nothing. The burning fire in my chest that had kept me motivated faded, as if the darkness around had finally snuffed it out. My life felt meaningless.

"Tell me…" I turned with sudden childlike hope, "tell me that what you showed me is meant to intimidate me. Tell me that you're trying to terrify me. Please, I beg you."

I looked into what I imagined was the center of his eyes, searching for some sign that what he'd showed me was a dream. He stared back, the hint of a smile tugging at his cheek. I felt my world crash around me, like a bird shot through the heart.

"Your family is dead." His words slammed the last nail in the coffin of my life.

I sank back onto the hooks beneath me, and the pain which had hounded me in the background of my mind faded to the emotional deadness I felt. I no longer felt like enduring the torment he brought on me. My friends and family had died, and I had not been there for any of them. Every one of them had come to trust that I would deliver them from the death sentence inflicted on them, but instead I'd lead them like cattle to an abattoir.

"Do what you will with me," I heard myself say.

I no longer cared what happened; in fact, I welcomed the sweet peace of death. At least then I'd be with those I loved instead of shackled to a torture bed where my blood and tears spilled side by side.

My skin prickled, and I straightened my back reflexively. Without willing it to, my right arm raised, and in a powerful jerk, the chains holding it down snapped in two. I blinked rapidly and tried to stretch my fingers, but they wouldn't respond. My head turned to the left and I struggled to move any part of me. My left arm, of its own will, sent the chains holding it down flying into the darkness. I sat up in the same moment as I willed myself to remain down.

"Finally!" But the words from my lips were not my own. I felt like I was watching through someone else's eyes as my arms reached down and rent the shackles on my legs till they tore free. As if strings were attached to my body and a puppet master moved the controls, I swung my legs over the side of the platform and stood. With an internal shiver, I realized I was not alone in my body. Another dark force brooded, unwelcome, in the deep recesses of my soul.

"Yes, Phoenix," the feeling inside me murmured, and though it was me who murmured the words and yet not me at all. "The time has come to return home. You have fulfilled the words spoken of my return."

I turned and stared down and for the first time saw the bed I'd lain upon. The jagged edges of the hooks held clumps of my skin. Beneath them a trough of liquid sat concealed in the darkness. I leaned forward and sniffed. The aroma of blood assailed my nostrils, and had I been in control of myself, I'd have thrown up. I glanced at a crumpled body next to the bed, and with a jolt I realized it was Mordën, motionless. I smiled and turned. Raul stood at the door, his face ashen as he spotted the corpse on the ground and the broken chains.

"How... uh, how did you escape?"

"Calm yourself, Raul, it is I."

"Master?" Raul's eyes widened with first horror and then worshipful love as he dropped to his knees. "It worked? The prophecy came true?"

I reached a hand and stroked his bald head. "We are going home, Raul."

Raul took my hand and kissed it. In another life, the scene would have been comical, a grown man blubbering over the fingers of a child. Now it possessed a sinister aspect as I reached my hand around, expecting to feel the holes which the hooks had left in me. The flesh had already begun to knit itself together, and soon I felt nothing but smooth skin. Blood returned to my veins and I breathed back the life I'd lost.

"Take me to the Pit," I said.

Raul hurried from the room, and I followed. We journeyed down a dimly lit, crudely built tunnel until it opened into a wide room. At one end, the floor vanished into a space the size of a casket and six feet deep. I knelt at the edge and spoke a soft chanting melody. The aged stone base glowed, and a white sheen glossed the floor until it vanished. Beneath it, a brilliant white light glowed. I turned back to Raul, who stood like a proud mother.

"My liege, Black Widow," he beamed, "you return to avenge those who so cruelly dismissed you?"

"I'm no longer the Black Widow," I murmured and glanced at my fingertips as I stood and stepped over the edge of the pit. "I'm Mordën, Lord of Death, Heir to Ëone."

Epilogue

A soft wind brushed my nose and I smiled. Eyes shut and lying prone on my back, I heard the sounds of waves crashing on a beach followed by the faint cries of a bird soaring overhead. A warmth, which only the sun could provide, moved through my body, preparing the aching joints in my body. I chuckled gently and rubbed my eyes. I was at peace.

A cool point prodded my chest, and in an instant, my eyes flew open and I was on my feet, hand reaching for my waist. A dark shape of a man towered in front of me, a longsword gripped in one hand. A bow slung over his shoulder, he stared at me with distrust in his golden eyes. He took the sword in both hands and pointed it at me, firming his stance. Behind him a black horse snorted and stamped the ground.

"Who or what are you?" He said, his voice raspy and deep. "You are no shade nor do you bear the mark of the Varg." He narrowed his eyes and took a hesitant step forward.

I made a great show of holding both hands up and displaying all of my fingers. I did my best to conceal the shaking in my hands as I opened my mouth. I closed it as I realized I had no answer. My memory consisted of the warm sunlight and the crashing waves mere moments prior.

"I don't know." My own words seemed alien to me. "I remember the beach, the feeling of the sun, and the scream I heard a scream."

"A scream?" The man's face scrunched in confusion.

"I… don't know." My eyes widened as I looked around me, soaking in the scenery I'd described. To the right a great ocean stretched against the horizon. To my left an extensive grassland, sunny plains and rolling hills extended out of sight as they met with the cloudy sky. The vista seemed divided—a white glow suffused the land while a brooding blackness hung over the waters.

"What is your name?" I asked. "Where am I?"

"Shall I name myself before I know if you are friend or foe?" The man grimaced. "Surely one who has ventured this far east from Avalon knows the lands he travels."

"I *don't* know."

I turned and stared toward the rolling waves and the dark foreboding deeps of the ocean. The fitful winds were heavy with the scent of the surf, and the waves forked and burst into the sky in a fierce passion. The choppy waters tumbled over each other as they broken upon several massive boulders set like monstrous teeth along the shore.

"My name is DarSheer," the man said. "A member of the Outpost."

"The Outpost?" I shook his hand though alarm bells rang in my head. "I swear I know naught of anything since… you said I fell from the sky?" I wrinkled my brow and shook my head.

"You must have inhaled the fragrance of some hag's potion or dallied in the taverns longer than you should have," DarSheer eyed me as if I were about to scream and jump at him.

"The taverns?" I wrinkled my nose. "What business would I have in a tavern? I swear this oath to you, I remember nothing past laying here on this grassy knoll and feeling the unwelcome blade you carry prick me. Wait…"

I felt a pounding headache as a single name popped to the forefront of my memory. I slammed my fists into my temple and dropped to one knee. DarSheer rushed to my side, hand supporting my shaking arm.

"What ails you?" He helped me to my feet, and we began to move slowly toward his mount.

"A name I remember a name!" I breathed as the headache became unbearable. An ache seemed to split my head in two as I fell forward onto the grass. I thrashed amongst the plants as the name burned into my core.

"You're ill," DarSheer hoisted me up onto the saddle and vaulted up behind me. "The outpost is not far, and their healers are the most learned for leagues around."

"Get it out of my head," I moaned as we began to gallop north along the beach's edge.

I am restored—a voice spoke soothingly into the emptiness of my head.

I gasped, my eyes squeezed shut. "He's here."

"Who?" DarSheer rode confidently and if my strange behavior unnerved him he made no sign.

I opened my eyes and felt an inexplicable dread wash over me.

"He's here. Mordën has returned."

▲▼▲▼▲

About the Author

Born in 1998 and once a resident of California, **Robert Scheck** currently lives in Colorado, under the watchful eyes of the Rocky Mountains.

After being entertained by the great fantasy works of Tolkien, Lewis, Mull, Rowling, and Martin, Robert decided to embark on a great journey himself into the world of fantasy.

He currently works hard on the trilogy *A Tale of Blood and Tears*, *Shadowed Time* being the first of this trilogy.

With plans of many literary quests to come, he has no desire to put the pen down anytime soon and considers the following fact dear to his heart: *behind every author, there resides a mighty force of loyal readers.*

It is his dream to finish his trilogy and give back to the world of fantasy fiction for all the countless hours of joy it gave him.